MARSHALL CAVENDISH CLASSICS

SEVENTEEN

T0166726

Seventeen

COLIN CHEONG

Marshall Cavendish
Editions

© 2021 Colin Cheong and Marshall Cavendish International (Asia) Pte Ltd

First published in 1996 by Times Editions

This edition published in 2021 by Marshall Cavendish Editions
An imprint of Marshall Cavendish International

A member of the
Times Publishing Group

Other Marshall Cavendish Offices:
Marshall Cavendish Corporation, 800 Westchester Ave, Suite N-641, Rye Brook, NY 10573, USA • Marshall Cavendish International (Thailand) Co Ltd, 253 Asoke, 16th Floor, Sukhumvit 21 Road, Klongtoey Nua, Wattana, Bangkok 10110, Thailand • Marshall Cavendish (Malaysia) Sdn Bhd, Times Subang, Lot 46, Subang Hi-Tech Industrial Park, Batu Tiga, 40000 Shah Alam, Selangor Darul Ehsan, Malaysia

Marshall Cavendish is a registered trademark of Times Publishing Limited

National Library Board, Singapore Cataloguing in Publication Data

Name(s): Cheong, Colin.
Title: Seventeen / Colin Cheong.
Other title(s): Marshall Cavendish classics.
Description: Singapore : Marshall Cavendish Editions, 2021. | First published in 1996 by Times Editions.
Identifier(s): OCN 1253290271 | ISBN 978-981-4974-51-6 (paperback)
Subject(s): LCSH: Junior college students--Singapore--Fiction. | Youth--Singapore--Fiction.
Classification: DDC S823--dc23

Printed in Singapore

Frame S

Sunday, May 10, 1987

The wind breathes and pictures move.

Photographs float like sepia leaves, scratching along the red-bricked ground, scattered like cards in a giant game of memory.

Voices gather, movement blurs, shadows flit along the corridors — a homecoming to a deserted building. People huddle in small groups for the camera, smiling on reflex, making memories of their own while memories of past generations drift around their feet.

Some stop to look, to touch, but no one ever taking the old pictures because the moments are not their own. I bend to catch a leaf floating past. Veined with creases, it shows old young faces smiling between the lifelines, product of a photosynthesis that gives life to matter, life to memory.

The wind sighs again, and the old pictures rustle on the floor, images of us, images of time measured in fractions of a second, the sum of which might have never made a minute. But there are images we never catch on film, leaf-pressed in the pages of the heart, dodged and burned to fit the reality we prefer to remember.

But even memory on a postcard print is brittle. The leaf is beginning to brown. A print made by beginners' hands, perhaps even my own. These hands are unfamiliar now. A few short years have written more lines on them than I care to read. The photograph slips from my fingers and it dances away on the wand, a decisive moment shared.

And that is why I tell this story now. Because it is vivid still, fresh and unmanipulated, but fragile, like all things we hold only in our minds and even the foundations of this school building. I want to tell it before the illumination of age burns all away to shadow and tells me such a story could only be a tale from a Chinese studio.

The old Seagull rangefinder hangs from my shoulder. I brought it hoping to take something away with me too, something missed when I was last here, an image of a moment to share with a stranger who could be me years from now, who might not know the boy.

And what would the boy tell the man?

My school was going to fall like a house of cards. They made everyone leave on Friday, but over the weekend, we went back, hundreds of us, not just present pupils, but old ones, like me. We went home to say goodbye.

Wasn't that a dangerous thing to do? The man might ask and I can see no answer for a rational adult.

But I could put between us a deck of pictures, my postcard moments, hot-pressed, heart-pressed, turning each one over, letting him read the past from those browning leaves.

And I could hope old eyes would see what young eyes understood.

Frame 1

The light is harsh now, at three o'clock, and darkness will be a long time coming. I sit on the steps of the forum and look out at the plaza where we used to assemble in the morning, the left and right wings of the main building, like the arms of a protective mother, encircling her brood.

I remember being told that, but I cannot see the councillor telling me. Trying to remember moments, all I can call to mind are pictures. Everything else between pictures — as if we never were. And so we cheat. We remember things, but never in the way they really were, dodging our inadequacies, burning out the pain. And cheating could begin even in the camera. Darkroom work only confirms what you want to believe and the print is not disputed.

The plaza is quiet now, the babble of souvenir hunters starting to fade with the light, but if I can recall enough details to fill in the blank, the space will live again. The people in my picture move, fidgeting in their lines, picking up files, dropping bags, waving. The babble swells again, speakers hiss, a teacher orders *maktab*, *sedia* and the school band strikes up *as part of our glorious land, sharing her spreading fame, Hwa Chong will firmly stand* ... The irony is not lost on me.

Across a school field, traffic rumbles down Bukit Timah Road and there is the sharp smell of exhaust that always brings back pictures of sunlight in the trees around the field, shining off the beige walls of the college buildings, the stylised Chinese characters on the balustrades shadow sharp. And the feeling then that everything is good and exciting and new.

I close my eyes to see it better.

Frame 2

Tim and me, walking down Orchard Road, O-level results in our pockets, feeling good. Tim's got 14 points, a miraculous 10 points down from his prelims and he's going to Catholic. I've got 10, seven points down from prelims. I'm going to Catholic too. Where the Convent girls are, Heaven is too. But Tim is telling me maybe Catholic isn't such a good idea. Maybe I should be going someplace I can get help with Chinese as a Second Language.

I'm a provisional. That means I didn't pass Chinese at O-level and I'd better clear it on either of my next two tries or I'm out of junior college. And without a junior college pass in Chinese, I won't get past the pearly gates of the local uni.

Go Hwa Chong, Tim says. Your Chinese is sure to improve in a Chinese school. You can't score without it. You'll have to learn.

What? Go to that commie tok-tong-chang school where all they do is lion dance and sing songs of the Yellow River? Where every other bloke thinks he's a monk of the Shaolin Temple? No way, man. It's too radical an idea to accept, I tell him.

Uni or girls, man, you have to choose, Tim says.

I think he just wants to keep the Convent girls all to himself.

But what Tim says stays in my mind and in an awful way I know that he is right, because if I don't get help, there's no way I can clear the repeat exams short of cheating. And I remember a catechism teacher warning me that the trail to Heaven is steep and rocky but the highway to Hell is wide and easy.

Maybe it is Tim's logic. Maybe it is my Catholic sense of guilt and need to do penance in a personal hell. Maybe it's the seductive irony of being a Chinese failure in Hwa Chong. Maybe I think I just can't score with Convent girls anyway. In any case, at the tender but turgid age of sixteen, I wisely choose my educational future over Convent girls.

Frame 3

"*Zhao an*." My voice is hesitant, my intonation poor.

"It's all right. We speak English here."

"Thank God."

"What's your name?"

"Richard Young. Is this A11?"

"You're ours. Okay people, this is Richard. Hey, isn't the rest of your name here too?"

"That's it. All of me. There's no more."

"Really?"

"Really." Something in my voice tells the councillor that I am tired of being asked that question. All my life, harassed by chauvinistic Chinese teachers who think it is disgraceful that a Chinese boy should have no Chinese name, who tell me that I am a banana, yellow outside and white inside because I speak English better than them, I'm Catholic and I have no Chinese name. Tired. The councillor smiles.

"Well. I'm Samantha Loh and that's it too. I'm your class councillor. Now take a seat while I sort your t-shirts."

First day in school. I sit down and look around. A first-year cohort of junior college students is a sight to see.

Coming from schools all over Singapore, they move like a wave of immigrants in their ethnic colours at the start of every school year, crisscrossing the island in search of a new home, their O-level aggregates their passports.

They arrive at junior colleges in their old uniforms to form a giant human quilt of every fade and shade of white, blue, green, maroon, yellow, brown, grey and pin-stripes and polka dots, eventually settling and taking on the hues of their new homes. A girl in a uniform with green polka dots and a fake green tie comes up to shake hands.

"Welcome to the class. I'm Janice. I'm class rep and that's Jacqueline, the pretty one with long hair, she's assistant class rep."

Before I can say thanks, she is waving for the quilt patches to gather for introductions.

"That's — *everything in between is a blur* — Got that?"

"Uh-huh." I say, and it is all I manage to squeeze in between Janice's rapid-fire words.

There is a chorus of hi, hello, happy to have you here as Janice goes on and the sound cuts only when Samantha throws me a set of Hwa Chong t-shirt and shorts and yells for the class to get changed in three minutes for Orientation II games.

As the class groans with Janice shouting can't we orientate the bloke ourselves and Sam singing back no, I suddenly realise that the only Chinese spoken has come from my own lips. And there are no Convent girls in my class.

But there is Samantha Loh.

As our class councillor, Samantha is our senior. She is in the Oxbridge class. She lives at Cairnhill and went to Singapore Chinese Girls' School.

She isn't really pretty or anything, but she's sweet and fair and her cheeks go rose when we say things that make her blush, which is very often. Her hair is brown in the light and her eyes are hazel and her lashes long. You don't notice all this until she takes off those big plastic-framed glasses she wears. She's tall and thin and our class people say that if you put her in a floral print dress, she'd look like an economics tutor.

But I don't care.

She talks sweetly and gently enough to me, even though what we say to each other never goes further than idle-forum chatter. If she taught me economics, I would Ph.D. in it just to be near her for as long as possible. And then I would feel smart enough to ask her out.

ZZ thinks I'm nuts. I agree.

Frame 4

ZZ, or Zhuang Zi, is my best friend in college, bestest ever friend a guy could have and you know how rare that is among males past puberty.

We meet shortly after Orientation II ends, when the Photographic Society holds a recruitment exhibition in the forum. I've always been into photography, reading anything I can get my hands on about it, collecting catalogues and wishing I had a camera, any camera, just so that I could at least start making pictures.

So Janice, Jacqueline and me — they've taken me under their wing after Orientation II — go have a look and I'm filled with bitter envy, thinking all the time that I can make better pictures but for the money.

Then this voice behind me asks, hey want to join the club?

And I say, without even looking back, no, I don't have a camera.

Don't worry, the voice says, the club has cameras you can use and only then do I turn around and look at the voice. Janice lends me the five dollars to sign up for membership and the beginner's course.

The voice is tall, skinny — pale from the long hours

in the darkroom. A Chinese High boy, total opposite of my Catholic Joe. He talks in a lazy, easy way and you can't help but like him because he has no ego. I never know his grades until I really know him, which is rare in a place like Hwa Chong. He also makes the worst coffee in the world and club members call it D-76, after the developer we use.

After the basics course, we share the darkroom, just the two of us, because no one else fancies hanging out all day in a red-lit sardine can that smells of D-76, hands soaked in all kinds of poison. And because there really isn't anything else to do while waiting for things to develop or dry, we sit around and talk and become great pals.

I guess the greatest things a teenaged boy can have is somewhere to run to and a friend to run there with.

We both have problems at home. ZZ's family has expectations of him — even his name is supposed to be that of some famous Chinese scholar — and my mother has expectations of my father and I am basically invisible anyway and you know how all this leads to problems that never get sorted out.

So the darkroom is a sanctuary for the both of us. It's a great little place. There are shelves, a radio, a kettle, a table-top refrigerator, air-conditioner and a couple of thin mattresses that when you lay them end to end, take up all the floor space in the lab.

It's so comfortable that we spend a lot of time there, either developing negatives or making prints or just doing our homework. It beats anything at home, mine at least. And ZZ is an ace in Chinese and helps me no end in getting my assignments done (so Tim is right after all).

If ZZ, as photo society chairman, had managed to get an attached shower in there, I would have never gone home again. We had everything but the girl.

Frame 5

Everything but the girl. Yes, there are girls, but they aren't ours.

Sam leans on the concrete rail and the wind catches her hair just as she turns towards me and smiles when she sees the camera against my face.

Hey don't you dare, she laughs, but the click has come and gone. My first and only picture of her.

Later in the lab, my fingers tremble in the darkness as I unload that precious latent image, feeding it into the spool, dropping it into the developing tank and then sealing it tighter than is necessary.

ZZ supervises the developing of the negatives and when they are done, I can hardly wait for the strips to dry. When they finally do, I hold one strip to the light, eyes fixed on one beautiful rectangle frame of translucent tones that shape Sam's face and smile. But she is still one step away from reality.

In the glow of the safelight, ZZ sets up the enlarger, slots in the negative strip, frames a piece of glossy paper in the easel, eight inches by ten, and doesn't even remind me to make a test strip.

I make the exposure, my first print, and ease the

paper into the developer. It sits in the solution, nothing happening at first, and then the darker tones begin to appear, gaining in strength, then forming into masses, dark and light patches slowly gaming substance and relating to form a two-dimensional, tonal representation of Sam.

And she is still one step away from reality.

Two other people know about this thing I have for Samantha. They are Janice and Jacqueline, my class reps. They think it's hilarious and every day, they scheme to get Sam and me to talk or get her to sit with us in the canteen. Jac even copies Sam's timetable when she leaves her file in the forum with us.

It makes us very close, and I have never had girls as close friends before. It feels different and nice, because you can tell girls things you wouldn't want to tell another guy, unless he was someone like ZZ. Very soon, I don't even think of Janice and Jacqueline as girls. They are just my friends and that's pretty much good enough for me.

Janice is tiny, but she packs a lot of energy, and she's always leading, always has ideas and always has guts for anything. About the only thing she doesn't have is doubts. Jacqueline and I let her boss us.

Jac's more laid back. She's tall and tanned and leggy. She outruns all the boys in the Arts Faculty, myself included. She's pretty too and people are always coming up to me to talk about her. I've threatened to sell her phone number, but I'm afraid she'll kill me if I do.

And then, there's Molly. Ha-ha. Molly is the girl who

likes ZZ and whom ZZ doesn't even notice. She's the only girl in the photo society and I suspect she joined because she likes ZZ.

She isn't at all bad-looking and I keep asking ZZ how come he won't be anything more than just polite to her. He says he just isn't interested. When I press him to go out with her, he says she's not very interesting. And then he asks me to go out with her.

Of course I say no, "because there's only room enough for Samantha in my heart."

If there was no Sam, would you go out with Molly?

I say of course not. I don't like Molly.

And he asks why not. So I tell him. I think Molly is neurotic. And she doesn't like me because I hang out with ZZ all the time. She's actually jealous, I suspect, because she has nothing nice to say about the pictures I take.

And you want me to go out with her?

You could be good for her.

I'm not here to save neurotic women from themselves, he says.

I tell him to give her a chance.

He tells me to give Jacqueline a chance.

That freezes me.

He tells me a relationship with Jac has far more going for it than one with Samantha because we're already good friends.

But the friendship's too good to risk, I say. And maybe its this running after Sam that keeps our relationship so good. We know where we stand with each other.

He asks me how I got to Hwa Chong. I do not appear to have too much brains. I get even by turning on the lights the next time he is making a print.

There are many rolls to process and we work late into the evening. ZZ hears it first, I guess, because he looks up from his cold D-76 with a frown. Then I hear them too, the first notes of a song on a bamboo flute, floating into our light-tight sanctuary.

It sings like the wind in the grass, shaking the leaves and stems of flowers, fluttering petals that call to the butterflies with their colour. Fragile notes dancing on air, lasting as long as their creator's breath, dancing in staccato steps or swirling pirouettes, making long leaps to high notes, and then trailing, fading, a steady stream of air dissipating into nothingness and silence.

What in hell was that? I ask.

Sounds like heaven to me, ZZ replies. He packs up, throws me the darkroom key and tells me to lock up.

Frame 6

It has to come, sooner or later. Remedials. In a stuffy classroom in Haw Par Building, the Chinese teacher stares at me. There is no one else to look at. It is only her and me. Everyone else's Chinese is better than mine. The walls are off-white and the paint is peeling in places. Outside the louvred windows are the grass and the tops of trees in the afternoon sun. One floor below, I can hear the creak and clink of gym equipment.

Do you know how to do the exercise?

I cannot read it.

You are not trying. You must try.

I really cannot.

Your Chinese cannot be so bad.

But it is.

No, don't be silly you must try.

She is a kind woman. And patient too. But she does not understand. I really cannot read it. And if I cannot read it, I cannot do it. Ten years of second language education have passed me by, the undetected illiterate.

I can hear the echo of voices from the forum where my classmates are. The school day is over and they are sitting around to talk, preparing to go for games. And I am sitting in a stuffy classroom alone with a Chinese teacher and an exercise I cannot do because I cannot read.

It seems like forever before we finish the exercise — and it's multiple choice. I think the lesson's over, but Miss Chan asks for the composition she set me the last lesson. I take out the one I have been writing for the last few exams.

My Chinese compositions all have different beginnings, but the story and endings are always the same. The beginnings, of course, are never mine. They are written by Chinese teachers who set test and exam papers. Even so, those beginnings are kind of the same. They are always dark, because where vision ends, imagination begins. It is always a sound that intrudes, because while eyes may be closed and focused elsewhere, ears may not.

So anything the teacher sets leaves my hero awakened, alerted, alarmed, on the edge of an extraordinary event. Imagination I have. It's just words I don't. My plot around that complication is to prepare a story memorise it and then adapt it crudely to fit any introduction a Chinese teacher might invent.

The standard story goes like so: once alerted, Hero moves from his one-room housing board flat into the Darkness. There, he performs a Brave Act, like Saving a Life. Then, the person saved introduces himself as a Messenger from the Netherworld — either an Old Man (representing wisdom) or a Young Boy (innocence, what else). The message is always from the Hero's Late Lover,

23

telling him to forget her and get on with his life in the world of the living.

Miss Chan is not amused.

But I think it is a great story.

No wonder you always fail Chinese, says ZZ.

Frame 7

The next time I meet Jacqueline, I remember what ZZ says about her being a better choice than Samantha and I am very nervous. Not because I want anything from her, but because I'm no longer sure if she wants nothing but my friendship. All 17-year-old boys presume too much.

We're sitting in the forum late in the afternoon, after my Chinese remedial is done. Janice is off somewhere in the field playing softball and so it's only the two of us.

"You okay?" she asks after a few lines of stilted conversation.

"I'm recovering from my Chinese lessons."

"How's it going?"

"Not well."

"Poor baby. Tell you something funny."

"What?"

"Tuck's got the hots for Jan."

At first, the thought of it tickles, until I realise that might leave Jac and me pretty much alone together. Everything's been in balance, like a nice equilateral triangle, but this would put the two of us on either end of the same line, drawing closer or further apart.

"You're not serious." I say at last.

"I am," she says, smiling.

"How is she taking it?"

"I think she's taking him."

"Holy cow. I suppose I'm Pageboy and you're Bridesmaid?"

She laughs, and for the first time, I realise how much I like the sound of her laughter. Oh, the power of suggestion. She brushes her veil of hair back and smiles. Then she speaks, and her voice is more serious.

"And when do you plan on asking Sam out?"

Long sigh.

"ZZ says passing my Chinese is more likely than that ever happening."

"Don't be so negative, Richard. The problem is you thinking it's impossible."

"So I should keep chanting I think I can I think I can?"

She laughs again. "Like the Little Blue Engine."

"I think I can I think I can I think I can."

"And very soon it's possible."

"Probably."

She puts her arm around me and my shoulders tingle at her touch, then suddenly the warm, soft weight of her arm is gone and her fist lands squarely on my shoulder.

"Don't give up so easy."

The shadows are long on the ground when we walk home. I have never liked the evening light, but this time, it seems bearable. I almost don't mind going home.

Frame 8

There are reasons why a boy doesn't want to go home. When I am seventeen, the only thing poorer than my Chinese is the English-educated family, which has of late, come down in life. This, in itself, might not be a big deal, but it colours the family portrait in a way that makes me want to stay out of the house as much as possible.

The father is a failed businessman, and the mother, a failed housewife. It is shortly after my birth that he loses, in a series of bad deals, the money his father left him. The mother, who married into money, has not learnt to adapt, and as the father's fortunes haven't recovered, neither has their relationship.

They have a precious firstborn son, raised in the time of plenty and an adored only daughter who also has the luck of being the youngest child. Henry is a thug used to getting his own way and the larger portion of anything or I eat his fist and lose everything. Elizabeth never crosses him either, instead turning her cheek on me because she knows I will not slap it.

The family lives in a cramped, single-storeyed terrace house in the Gardens where we fight each other for elbow room amid the cardboard cartons of hardware odds and ends spilled over from the father's shop in Paya Lebar. About the only time we do not fight is Sunday, when there is a tacit truce and we go to Saint Francis Xavier's for Mass. The father goes out of habit, the mother goes to keep up appearances, the brother and I go to look at girls and the sister, who has just turned 13, has also discovered boys.

We always walk to church, although at our pace, it takes nearly half-an-hour. The father says it is because parking is difficult. The brother says parking was not a problem when we still had the Benz.

By sundown, patience wears thin and the first stray shots are fired and our normal week begins by the nine o'clock news on Sunday night. I sometimes roll up my mattress and retreat to sleep in the quiet darkness of our beat-up panel van.

So, come daylight, I try to spend as much time as possible out of the house. I can just manage lunch and dinner out if I don't buy soft drinks or eat meat. There is never too much to eat at home anyway and if I don't show my face at bedtime and breakfast, they might forget about my existence altogether as I don't figure on the marketing bill.

The brother is happy about it. He can screw his girl-friend in our room. The mother does not mind because it means one less child to yell at. The sister does not care and the father never knows what is happening at home anyway (he's a bed and breakfast kind of guy too).

School for me then, has always been a refuge until

twilight, when the light steals away from the air, making long shadows on the ground. Then I feel my spirit slip away with the light, leaving me listless as I head home. I want a way to shut out that miserable half-light, that neither here nor there time of day between light and night when I have to leave school and head for home, the darkness of sleep and a panel van still far away.

But now, even school is becoming less of a refuge, because the Chinese monster has found me hiding there, found my hiding place in the darkroom. And if I cannot kill it, it will take my hiding place from me and I will have nowhere to hide, nowhere to run to. I don't want to go home and if I can't hide in school until I'm ready to leave home, there is nowhere else to go. And that makes me afraid.

Frame 9

This is not real, I declare one night in the darkroom. ZZ is working through a physics tutorial while I try to write a Chinese essay on filial piety.

"How do I write about filial piety when I don't even like my own parents?"

No need to be sincere, ZZ offers.

"Even a hypocrite needs to fill 400 squares with words and I don't have the words. This is like making me play Scrabble without vowels."

"Maybe you could start with a story of filial piety and then write the essay around it."

"I don't know any."

"Don't joke. Didn't you learn any during Chinese lessons in the last 10 years? The Chinese invented filial piety."

They may have, but half my mind shuts down when I hear Chinese and the other half shuts when I think the subject is filial piety. I hate preaching and hate it more when it is in Chinese.

ZZ thinks for a bit and then offers me a tale. I can no longer recall his exact words, but this is more or less what he told me.

There was once a Son of Heaven who wanted a big bell made that would be heard for a hundred li. He wanted the bell's voice to be strengthened with brass, deepened with gold, sweetened with silver.

He ordered his best Mandarin, Kuan Yu, to make this bell. Kuan Yu called together the finest craftsmen and they worked for months and finally, the bell was cast.

But they failed not once, but twice, because gold would not unite with brass, silver would not be joined to iron. The Son of Heaven was angry and Kuan Yu was then warned that if he did not succeed on the third attempt, he would lose his head.

The Mandarin's daughter, the beautiful and virtuous Ko Ngai, heard about it and was deeply afraid. So she sold her jewels secretly and went to see an astrologer famed for always being right.

The old man looked at the stars. He looked at the charts. He looked at the books. Then finally, he said: Gold and brass will never wed, silver and iron will never embrace until the flesh and blood of a virgin is mixed with the metals in their fusion.

On the final casting, Ko Ngai went to the site with her servant girl, watching from a high balcony. As her father gave the order to cast, she leapt into the flood of molten metal.

All that was left of her was a shoe, caught by her servant girl as she tried to stop Ko Ngai from jumping.

But the bell was perfectly formed and when it was struck, it sang for more than a hundred li. And to all who heard it, the bell's voice wept Ko Ngai! And in between the chimes, a woman sighed hiai. They say it is Ko Ngai sobbing for her shoe.

"So, how do you write 'bell' in Chinese?" I ask ZZ. He laughs and throws me a dictionary from the shelf. He leaves the room a while later and I press on, trying to fill green squares that will tell the bell story in a hundred or so characters.

And then the first notes of the bamboo flute drift into the darkroom.

I have never been alone with the music. This is the first time, and a chill runs down my spine at its haunting voice. The flute goes on and I slowly relax in the clarity of the notes. Long and clear they sing, stepping lightly on the night air, drifting on the breeze. A beautiful, gentle, soothing sound and I close my eyes to take it in.

Where is ZZ? Is he listening to it too? The music comes every night, everytime we are in the darkroom till late. And it always comes just before we pack up to leave the college. I glance up at our made-in-China clock. Its luminous hands point nine.

Who plays it, so regularly and so late? Who else stays later than the two of us? I asked ZZ once and he shrugged his shoulders and said he did not know. He says he has heard the flute since his first year in Hwa Chong and has never bothered to look for its player. Something makes me shudder at the thought, that we are not alone and that there is someone else out there in the darkness who is more alone.

Then, just as suddenly as it begins, the flute-song ends, its trailing note dying with its creator's breath.

Frame 10

ZZ lives in an old townhouse in Cairnhill, the kind where you have to walk up a steep flight of steps from the pavement outside before you even get to the ground floor. Its post-war colonial yellow and there are cracks in the walls with black stuff and moss on it and bougainvillaea hanging over balustrades in green and fuchsia cascades. The tiles are painted and faded and there's a rusting swing that's been repainted over and over just outside the barred windows with bottle green panes.

He pushes open the swinging cowboy saloon doors and the first thing I notice as we step inside is the sunshine just falling from the roof like a waterfall of light. It is a light so beautiful I want to kneel and weep. Can we do pictures here? I plead with ZZ and he laughs and says sure, so long as nobody's home, which is just about never.

Only then do I notice the emptiness and silence of his hall, his narrow, deep hall with the shining dark red tiles on the floor leading up to the great polished wooden altar at the far side wall. You have ancestral tablets, I whisper and ZZ looks puzzled, probably wondering why that surprises me. But it does; it does, because ZZ is just not the kind of person you associate with old Chinese tradition and ancestral worship.

You a believer? I ask and ZZ nods. In spite of his Chinese High education and his sheer ace-ness at Mandarin, it has never occurred to me that ZZ even has a religion, let alone a Chinese one because he has always been a man of science to me. Man of science and reason. Even our hobby is all about light and optics and photo-chemical reactions.

My grandparents are upstairs and probably having their afternoon nap, ZZ says. It is so quiet in here I don't even answer, just nodding to everything he says. But I've forgotten the waterfall of light and my eyes are fixed on the pictures of people that line that altar wall, their names brushed in script I obviously cannot read. It has to be names — there are three characters. Chinese names always come in three characters — that is, if people have proper Chinese names, unlike me.

ZZ comes back from the kitchen with Cokes and we sit in his quiet, empty hall, cool because the ceiling is ever so far away and I feel really tiny in this great townhouse of ZZ's which looks so skinny from the outside. You never told me about you being an ancestor-worshipper I say and ZZ asks what's to tell? You don't talk about being Catholic either. Yeah, but I didn't expect you to be a believer, I say and ZZ wants to know why.

Because you're a man of science and reason, I tell him. Men of science and reason don't have religions, especially something so traditional. It would be believable if you believed in crystals or something, but ancestral worship is far too traditional.

ZZ laughs. Science hasn't got everything explained, he says. It really hasn't. There is so much we still don't know. And yes, it's true, I really believe in this. You know, we treat our ancestors as if they are still alive, like they are in the house right now.

It is broad daylight, but a chill runs up my spine and I whisper, like ghosts?

Spirits, ZZ answers. And spirits aren't all bad, like in the movies. I believe they are just like people, like you and me, a little bit of good and bad.

Am I being rude, I suddenly ask. If they are here like you say, should we even be talking about them like so?

ZZ laughs and shakes his head. They'll understand. You are not a believer and you will ask questions that would sound disrespectful if a believer asked.

So, uh, do they ever get mad at you, like your parents?

ZZ sighs. I guess. It's worse because I cannot hear them scold me, but my parents always remind me of how ashamed I've made them.

Why's that?

You know how I got my name right? Some old Chinese scholar? A name like that is hard to live up to. And whenever my grades or performance in anything is less than perfect, that's it. Man, Richard, if I was really as good as my name, they'd have no reason to be ashamed of me. When I told one of my teachers in Chinese High about my name, she laughed and said it was also the name of the man who didn't know if he was a man dreaming that he was a butterfly or a butterfly dreaming he was a man. And that's my problem. I'm a dreamer. And I can't live up to my ancestors' hopes.

And you can square trying to make your ancestors happy with all the science and shit you learn in school?

Like I said, we haven't got it all covered. Not everything. Lots of things we don't know or understand yet. Lots of principles, forces to learn about. It's like any other religion. It is only a hypothesis to explain certain phenomena we don't really understand fully. Our hypotheses give us a way of handling these unknown areas. It is exactly the same with Catholicism, don't you think?

I'm a cradle Catholic and yeah, also on Sundays.

ZZ laughs again. Well, it is a system of beliefs, right? You have a way of explaining how the world came to be, you have a story about God and his people and Jesus coming down and all, right? That's a hypothesis too.

Don't hypotheses have to be substantiated by empirical evidence? I am an arts student, but that doesn't mean I'm stupid. I know hypotheses need to be backed up with proof.

ZZ shakes his head. Every hypothesis has something to prove it, but not conclusively because we can never know everything. For every law proven right, there may come something later to prove it wrong.

It's a leap of faith, ZZ goes on. You can get all the evidence you want and it will never be enough to prove that God exists or my ancestors are in this room. Logic ends and then you have to jump that last bit to believe.

I don't think I ever had to jump to be Catholic.

Maybe you never gave it enough thought.

No man, I just grew up with it and I accept it like two plus two is four and the world is round. No leap of faith there.

Your faith strong?

It's a while before I can answer. No, it isn't. Haven't got much of it. It's kind of just there, like I know my parents had parents and they were rich one time. The knowledge doesn't change my life.

That's where we're different, ZZ smiles. I know my parents had parents and they were rich one time too and some of them are upstairs sleeping and the others are here too, watching over us as we talk.

About them, I say, clearing my throat and trying to sound polite about it.

You don't think my granny upstairs would come down and hit you for talking about her, would you? ZZ asks suddenly. I shake my head.

My granny who's gone but still here isn't going to hit you either. She's just like any granny. Just that she's gone but here. You get it?

I stare at the wall, the altar, the pictures, the can of Coke in my hand, hear the dong-dong-dong of the grandfather clock echo in the big hall and try to take it all in. I don't have any feeling about my own God being around, in person, not the way ZZ feels about his late grandparents and relatives whose pictures line the altar and the

37

walls. There is no leap of faith needed for me because I don't give religion much thought. It just isn't an issue. I go to church with the family on Sundays, in the same way I used to follow them to see Grandpa on Saturday nights. We're going off to see someone, we don't doubt his existence, we're not terribly excited about it, but it's something we always do, so get in the van and shut your face, we're going to see Grandpa or we're going to church, so hurry up.

It's like having another world right here in ours, I say at last.

That's right, ZZ replies. They can cross into ours, but we can't cross over into theirs.

Unless we're dead.

Unless we're dead, he nods.

No case for segregation?

What for?

What for indeed.

Frame 11

As we walk out into the evening light, ZZ suddenly turns to me and says, do you want to see where Sam lives? It's not even a question because he never gives me a chance to answer and drags me along by the elbow up and over the hill.

Of course I want to see where she lives. It's the same reason why people want to go on pilgrimages to the Holy Land. They never ever see Jesus or any of the apostles or even the Virgin Mary, but they go anyway. But I'm not hoping to see Sam. In fact, I'm very worried that she might see me.

So we're standing on holy ground and ZZ has his arms raised, saying here, here, your goddess lives here, bow down and worship. And I'm losing my nerve in front of that big grey condominium block with all the rich people living inside it and telling him to knock it off and let's get out of here before she sees us, but ZZ is laughing at me as I make a halfhearted attempt to push him away all the time, hoping hoping hoping that I get a glimpse of Sam without her noticing the two twits on her sidewalk.

Let's go, I say and he says now you know where she lives, you can come back anytime and you can drop by my place for a drink or catch some TV if you get bored or if your silly neck gets stiff.

What makes you think I'm that stupid, I ask and he laughs. Then I swear to myself that ZZ is never going to catch me on Sam's sidewalk.

Frame 12

And so the day of reckoning arrives. I go to the office and almost at once I know the results of my June attempt at Chinese. My Chinese teacher's face is saying sorry before I can even say *zhao an*, Miss Chan.

It shouldn't surprise me, but even the undeserving hope for miracles, that little bit of magic that makes life a little more bearable, that hints that maybe life has meaning beyond the mundane and material.

But I knew it was a very, very long shot the moment I turned over the exam paper. I want to cry now just as I wanted to then, facing a piece of paper that could have just as well been blank because I understood none of what was printed on it. Tears are not for regret, just despair.

Never mind. You have another chance in November, but you must work much harder to get ready for that. Miss Chan says and I wonder how much readier I can be by then.

Outside the office, in the forum, Janice, Tuck and Jacqueline are waiting.

Shall we observe a moment of silence, I say, trying to smile and Jac says oh no. She puts an arm around me and then the afternoon quiet is broken by a clash of brass and the hammering of wooden sticks on tightly-stretched leather as the lion dance guys start their weekday practice.

Damn, Janice says, but I don't feel any anger and just let the drumming and the smashing of the cymbals wash over me, a song of triumph for a loser too tired to be insulted.

It is almost forever before the lion dance guys take a break. I'm used to it because their room is around the corner from the lab where our darkroom is. I hated it at first, then just grew used to it, until now, when I don't even notice it anymore. If only the learning of a language and the absorbing of a culture were so simple. Simple as the whacking of the stubby wooden sticks on the stained leather, following a rhythm that becomes second nature with unconscious effort, following the repetitive logic of natural cycles, following in the pawprints of another dancing lion before you.

Thank God, they've stopped, Janice sighs. You know, it's almost soothing, in a way, I say. It blocks out everything else.

Jac hasn't said anything but in a funny way, I know it hurts her too and I find myself trying to cheer up just so she won't feel so bad.

Or maybe she knows there really isn't any hope for me, not now and not in November. She should know. She helps me do my homework after all.

I'm OK, I tell her, but she doesn't look convinced and I'm torn between telling all of them to leave me alone for a bit and just crying on Jac's shoulder (they're broad enough).

Hey, Sam's walking this way, Tuck whispers and I look up automatically and regret it the moment she sees me. With Jac's arm still around my shoulder. She comes over and asks, so did you make it? Then our faces make sense and she says I'm sorry. What's going to happen now?

I try again in November.

I'm sure you'll make it then.

Maybe.

You just have to work at it. Hey I've got a late class. Don't feel too bad. It isn't the end.

She walks away. Jac's had her arm around me all that time and I feel a flash of annoyance, but it goes as quickly as it comes.

Be brave, Jac says, smiling.

I'll try.

So, I ask Tuck, do you think Sam likes me?

Frame 13

ZZ is sympathetic until I get to the part about Sam coming up.

"You're a moron," he says in the total blackness of the darkroom as we load film into the developing tanks.

"Oh thanks, I really needed that."

"Not about the Chinese. Even I am more sensitive than that."

"Then what? It was stupid to tell Sam I'd flunked? How do you think I was going to hide that from her?"

"You're a moron. I'm not talking about your failure in Chinese. I'm talking about you and Sam."

"And?"

"You're a moron." He laughs in the dark.

"If I could see you, I'd hit you."

"Heh. You're definitely in the dark."

"You are not helping me get over a very miserable moment in my life."

"Richard, would you do Chinese if you didn't have to?"

It's funny, but at the beginning of the year I would have said no straight out. But now I can't.

"No," I say after awhile.

"Why not?"

"No point wasting time on a subject I can't pass."

"Would you do it if there were no exams?"

Again, I would have said no straight out it someone had asked me at the beginning of the year.

"I might," and my answer surprises me, like a stranger's voice in the dark. I can't explain. It has to do with ZZ himself and our friendship. My Chineseness goes as far as my skin, but ZZ's is deeper, like the lion dance drumming that no longer sounds alien or threatening, like the way we say our college name with Chinese intonation, like the way the flute sings the place to sleep at night. And then I realise how much being at Hwa Chong has changed my attitude to things Chinese. I thought I would hate everything more, but I haven't. I still don't love it, but I don't hate it anymore, accepting it all as part of my surroundings.

"Because you're here and because I'm here," I say at last and wonder if it makes any sense to him.

"That's good. It means your heart is open."

"Are you trying to be profound?"

"I don't have to try."

"So what are you getting at?"

"I'm sorry Richard. Sorry that a stupid exam stands between us. Actually, I think you would love Chinese if you studied it for fun."

"Hey we can still be friends."

He chuckles.

"It's so weird how your Chinese problem parallels your love life."

"Waddaya mean?"

"Think of relationships as something difficult, like learning a new language — in your case, Chinese. See, Sam is like a Chinese course with an exam at the end of it. Bad news for you."

"And how do you suggest making Chinese fun?"

"Don't you think you should enjoy the development of a relationship? Being friends, getting closer and all that?"

"Oh yeah. Learning Chinese from you is much more fun."

"Ah, you see. So how come you don't see in real life?"

"You lost me there."

"Jacqueline."

"Jac? Her Chinese is only slightly better than mine."

"No. Pursuing Sam is like studying for a Chinese exam. Pursuing Jacqueline is like studying Chinese because you want to understand songs and movies without subtitles."

"If you like her that much, I could always set you up." It's funny talking in total darkness. You can say anything because your voice doesn't even sound like it belongs to you. It just sort of hangs there in the nothing and you don't know if the words are reaching anyone.

ZZ laughs at my suggestion. And something in his laugh tells me that it isn't the idea making him shy. He is laughing to himself, as if I've made a private joke I don't understand myself.

"Really. It would be great. Two of my bestest friends in love." It isn't me speaking. The idea isn't even mine. But the voice is just hanging there, free to explore possibilities I would have never verbalised myself in the light.

"I don't think you'd want that."

"Why not?"

"Because she's yours."

"She's my friend. We're really good friends," my voice says. And we're not going to screw it up by going any further.

"Sometimes friends are afraid to get closer because they think it's going to mess up everything," he says.

"That's a good enough reason."

The lids screw down on the tanks, the D-76 sloshing inside them.

"Ready?"

"Sealed. Lights on."

The study lamp comes on and fills the room with a warm, cosy light.

"Richard, it's a nice feeling to love somebody and it's even nicer when they love you back."

"Says the expert. Since when did you find out all this?"

"I know."

"Well, I know too. It's a nice feeling to love Sam." Something catches me. No, it is not true. I don't love Sam. I could have said it in the dark. But not with the lights on.

"I don't think you love Sam."

No, I don't. You can't love someone you don't talk to seriously. You can't love someone you hardly know. And the only thing we have in common is that she doesn't have a Chinese name either.

"No, I don't."

"So what's your problem?"

"I don't know."

"Infatuation."

"Shaddup."

"Puppy love."

"I'm not thinking about it."

"Definitely not. There's no reason why you like her other than because she was your councillor, she's quite nice, she's quite cute."

"And the way she looks when she's studying and has her glasses on the tip of her nose."

"You're in love with an image, not a person."

I keep quiet and let that sink in. ZZ is right. There is really no reason why I like Sam other than the way she looks, her mannerisms and the way she talks. She is sweet, sheltered and scholarly. Everything I am not.

"You know how images work? They're symbols for something. Maybe Sam represents something you wish you had."

"Or want to be."

"Because you think it will make you happy."

"Oh."

"Think about it carefully."

ZZ turns the developing tanks over. I find my voice.

"Isn't it good to want something like what Sam represents?"

"Which is?"

"Normality?"

"From whose point of view?"

I don't know anymore. ZZ sighs and puts a hand on my shoulder.

"Richard, your thing for Sam is not going anywhere. I won't trivialise it by calling it a crush. You go and decide that for yourself."

"But you think that's all it is?"

"Yes. And you should get real about it soon because I think there's someone who really cares about you."

"Other than you?"

"Yah," he smiles. "And she's waiting."

Frame 14

Jacqueline looks up as I approach our table in the forum. Every class has its table, unofficially claimed but recognised by everybody else. So I always know where to find my class people and today is no exception.

She smiles, like she always does when she sees me and I ask myself why I have never noticed that before. She pushes away some of the things in front of her to make some space for me. The table is long and empty but its the space in front of her she wants me to be. Am I reading far too much in all this?

Hi, how's your day been? she asks like in those old time American sit-coms when Daddy comes home and that is the first thing Mummy asks him.

Hello, I say and something sticks in my throat. I cough and sit down on the bench clumsily, a tingling rising from my fingertips to my shoulders.

What's with you? she smiles and I give her a silly grin and shake my head. All this takes no more than ten seconds, but it feels like a very long time.

I have no Chinese remedial today, I say, trying to sound as casual as possible. It is true too, I am not cutting classes. What's your afternoon like? I try to ask, but my voice comes out all wrong.

What did you say?

I clear my throat and ask again, what's on this afternoon?

Nothing, she says, track's been cancelled. Coach is sick.

Oh, I say and open my file for something to do, just so that I don't have to look at her. She doesn't say anything, but something hangs in the air between us, like, an unresolved chord with the pianist's hands just hanging over the keyboard.

She is beautiful. I've always known that for a fact, but I've never felt it. But I feel it now. Not just because her hair falls around her shoulders like an ebony wave, but because locks brush against my skin when the wind blows; not just because her eyes are gentle, but because they are gentle when they turn to me; not just because her lips are lovely in a smile, but because they share my joy.

And take the words right out of my mouth.

"So," she says, breaking the silence, "since you've got nothing to do and I've got nothing to do — shall we go see a movie?"

Frame 15

ZZ is overjoyed.

"So, how did the movie go?"

"Don't make a big deal out of it."

"No, no, this is a vast improvement over Sam. I'm so glad you took my advice."

"Yah, yah."

"Finally got the courage to ask someone out."

"Not quite."

"You mean?"

"No, not a class outing. She asked me. That's all."

"Wimp."

"Shaddup! At least we went out."

"Had a good time?"

"Like all the other times I've been with her."

"Nothing special this time? Hey it was a first time for you guys. Come to think of it, isn't this your first date with anyone?"

"Shut up, already!"

"Oh, the times they are a'changing."

And indeed they are. Something fundamental has changed in our relationship. Although nothing was said, we aren't just friends anymore. There are signs. For one thing, all through the afternoon, I never mention Samantha, not once, something I've never done before with Jac. Sam has always been there between us, either physically or as a subject of discussion. And another thing, while Jac still touches me, she does not hit me anymore.

Frame 16

We have been printing all afternoon and I've been keeping an eye on the clocks luminous hands. When it touches six, I start to pack up.

"Going off already?" ZZ asks. I smile.

"Jac's off the track about now."

He laughs.

"Dinner?"

"And a walk, maybe."

"How's it going?"

"Coming along."

"Good man."

"Good woman."

"It must be love. Hey, don't you even want to see your prints before you go? They're almost done."

He lifts them carefully out of the rinsing tank and clips them to the drying line.

"You've come a long way" he says. "You remember when you first joined?"

He studies my prints now, saying, your first pictures were good. You always got the right moment, your framing always just about right too. But the light was always missing.

Can't help that. Light isn't always in your favour when you shoot college events all the time, I reply.

It is true. The light is often missing. We shoot in late mornings, early afternoons, on overcast days, with flash because we have to get a decent picture for the school magazine, meaning sharply focused, well-exposed and action frozen clearly.

But you're starting to take risks, to shoot just for the light, ZZ continues. That's good. This is nice, he says, pointing to a narrow strip of grey in a middle of deep blacks top and bottom and in the grey, our volleyball team silhouetted warming up with the beams and girders of the stadium in the background. Hardly a sports picture, he laughs, but good.

"You're ready to move on. You should be shooting things other than college events."

"Yes, but I can only draw the cameras when there's an event on."

"You need your own equipment."

"ZZ, you know how it is."

"And so I do," he says softly. Then he goes to his haversack and draws out something encased in black leather.

"So I'm giving you this."

"What?"

"It's my first camera. Had to save pretty long to get it even though it cost only seventy bucks."

He hands it to me and I open the leatherette case. Inside is a silver and black rangefinder, with a seagull engraved on it and a pair of Chinese characters I cannot read.

"Hai-oh," ZZ says. "It means seagull. This is a really basic camera. Focus, shutter speed and aperture are all manual. No metering. But the 50mm lens is very sharp and opens up to f2.8. Speeds are from B to 1/250th. Just right for shooting with available light."

"ZZ, I can't take this from you."

"Don't worry. The manual is translated into English."

"That's not it. I mean, this was your first camera. This is too big a gift."

"No gift too big or too small when it comes from a close friend. It's yours."

The camera has a good weight to it, sitting in my palm. ZZ smiles. He knows I want it.

"Thanks, ZZ." I say hoarsely.

"You're welcome. Just take care of it, and take good pictures. And now there's Jac..."

We laugh and then, neither saying anything, we reach out to hug each other like in so many of our pictures of our athletes, except now there is no one to shoot our special moment for us, and I feel a sadness like I am saying goodbye to a devoted friend and brother, the way it is between all men when a woman comes to take one of them away.

"Guess I'll be seeing you less in here," he says.

"Nah, I'll have to print what I shoot."

"But not everybody else's pictures too. Hey this is always home to you and you can bring Jac in. I'll waive the rules.'

We laugh again. It is odd because even though we will

see each other everyday, something is different now and we will see each other far less, like all the time after six in the evening, when Jacqueline finishes training.

"You won't feel too lonely, will you?"

"Hey, I'm used to it."

I laugh. "Yes, and you have that bamboo flute player for company."

"And so I do," he smiles, "and so I do."

Frame 17

Jacqueline is waiting in the canteen, at the far end near the squash court and she waves to me as I trot down the stairs. I've been feeling sorry about deserting ZZ, but now my heart is suddenly light and my feet feel like they aren't touching the ground.

"Hi, I thought you'd forgotten," she says.

"No, of course not," I say and then remembering that I had forgotten before, when ZZ and I were deep in printing and the class was kept waiting for me.

"How was printing?"

"Great!" I decide to tell her about the Seagull later. "And how was training?"

"I can start really fast now," she says and then sort of smiles, as if she means something else.

"Where shall we eat?"

"We can take a stroll up to Farrer Park."

Wonderful girl, I think. With all the allowance I get, that's about all I can afford. And she knows it. She's been my friend for long enough.

We get up to go and maybe it's accidental, but both of us carry our bags on the outside and even though we aren't holding hands — yet — our shoulders touch and everytime we do, I fall in love with her a little bit more. We walk through the housing estate of kings and queens and coronations and duchesses and dukes, she my princess, me her frog who hasn't quite become a prince yet. It's a long, winding way but quiet, with only the sound of cars come home and children being called in for dinner. My heart skips a few beats and my mind skips a few steps ahead to wonder if all this will happen to us one day, when I get to leave home with Jac and together we'll make a home elsewhere for just the two of us and home will be someplace I actually want to return to because she will be there.

She smiles and asks, "What's on your mind?"

"Nothing." I say and she laughs.

"Come on, I won't laugh."

"You just did!"

"Tell."

"I can't tell. Not yet." No, not yet. It is all so far away and I really cannot tell, but right now, with her next to me, I can almost believe forever. She smiles, her long ponytail swaying behind her and its almost as if she knows.

"What's on your mind?" I ask.

"Dinner," she grins and runs ahead of me as the streetlamps come on.

Frame 18

Dinner done, we take another slow walk home to her flat in Holland Drive. She doesn't let me carry her bag, although I thought I saw her smile when I offered to take it.

You don't have to, she says, adding with a touch of defiance: I can take care of myself.

It's almost a challenge, almost daring me to say let me take care of you, but I dare not.

We talk some more about school, about our lessons and assignments and I tell her about the Seagull that is weighing down my bag.

Hey let me see, she says and I fish it out for her. In the streetlight, the silver top is deep, rich and she squints through the viewfinder.

So this is how you guys see the world.

I am surprised that she even says that. No one who doesn't shoot seriously really understands that a viewfinder is really another way of seeing the world. It isn't just a window, it is a whole new context, a whole new way of seeing things.

Can I click it?

Go ahead, it's empty.

She turns it at me and clicks and the shutter is almost silent.

There, she says, I shall remember you just as you are tonight.

Why just tonight?

Why not tonight? Is there going to be more?

Her serve, her challenge, her gauntlet thrown.

A giant flock of invisible birds is calling and calling and calling in a great tree at the junction. A sickle moon hangs in a deep blue sky with the neon lights of the shophouses standing still amid the swirling streaks of headlights, taillights and flashing indicators. The wind is blowing, wrapping around me like arms in an embrace and me wishing Jacqueline would do the same.

Is there going to be more? Yes yes yes I want to shout above the noise.

Turning to her, I put my arm around her shoulder and draw her closer and all the tautness in her runner's body suddenly goes tender. The wind blows her hair into my face as I say as gently as I can above the sound of birds and traffic and wind in the leaves and branches:

as many, as many as you'll allow.

Frame 19

"Isn't it about time for you to go?" ZZ asks late one after-noon during printing.

"I'm staying with you tonight. Jac's home already. She's got an assignment to finish."

"And you don't?"

"A Chinese assignment. She spent all of yesterday helping me with mine."

"Ah so. Good, we've got to clear quite a few rolls tonight. Up to it?"

"No problem."

So we mix up a fresh batch of chemicals and prepare a new set of strips for printing.

"Who shot this batch?" ZZ asks. I put the negatives to the light and recognise them as my own.

"Shot them for the drama people. Their play, *The Life and Death of Tong-ho*."

"Where did you shoot?"

"In the cemetery along Adam Road."

"What?"

"Cemetery. Adam Road."

"With a guy in an old Chinese costume? You must have shocked anyone who was walking around there."

"In broad daylight, lah."

ZZ laughs and prepares to make a print. We pick one of Tong-ho with a curved walking stick, shot from a low angle, with headstones in the foreground. It looks creepy in negative, black sky, grey stones. It will make a good poster picture, ZZ says.

But many prints later, we still haven't got it right and ZZ is puzzled. The headstones are not coming out properly, always too dark or too light, although the upper bit with the actor in costume and the sky and grass is turning out okay. The negative is fine, contrast is average, density is even. It should be printing well, I don't understand, he mutters. And I am surprised that ZZ hasn't found a way to make a good print yet. He always does.

Then we hear it, the voice of the bamboo flute and with the negative image of the stones enlarged on the easel and the rest of the room pitch dark, I feel a chill run up my spine and this time, it isn't a fleeting feeling.

ZZ tries again, but looks like he's in a hurry. Then he suddenly says, look, try and work it out. I need to go out for a sec. He waits until the test print is moved from the developer into the fixer before opening the door. But outside in the laboratory, it is already dark.

The music is still playing and I'm alone in the darkroom with the negative — my negative — of the headstones and Tong-ho. The stones glow back at me from the easel, black words turned white, and I drop a mask over them so that I don't have to look at them. Maybe we can just print the top bit, with Tong-ho and his stick standing in the long grass. It looks nice, and where the sky is, we can fit the title and all the other information. Anything, just so long as I don't have to be alone with those headstones.

Without moving the mask much, I reset the easel for another crop, make another exposure and dunk it into the developer. After three hours, I just want to stop looking at headstones and go home with a decent print the drama people can use.

The picture grows in the developer, and it has good tones, nice gradation, as far as I can tell in the safelight. And the composition is nicely balanced, though the drama of the headstones is lost. When the picture has gone through all the wet processes, I turn on the normal lights and it looks not just decent, but quite good.

Done it, I say almost in triumph and notice that the music has stopped for a while now. Then there is a rapping on the door. I call safe! and ZZ opens it.

He looks different, kind of flushed, and I notice that's how he looks everytime he comes back to the darkroom after being gone for awhile. Then I realise that he always leaves about the time the music starts and if he comes back, he comes back when it ends.

I have the solution, he says. I know how we can get a print.

I hold up mine for him to see. He cocks his head, stares at me and says, funny, but that was what I was going to tell you to do. Just crop away the headstones. Then his eyes light up in a funny way and he smiles and says, hey, let's call it a night, shall we?

Frame 20

You want to hear a true ghost story? I ask Jacqueline and she giggles yes, tell me. So I tell her about the darkroom and the night the headstones would not appear and her eyes grow wide.

Are you sure the negatives weren't wrong? she asks. No, no, no, we checked everything, even under the grain checker. It was fine and should have printed normally, the whole thing.

And only when we left out the headstones did the picture print properly you know, like as if the people whom the stones belonged to didn't want us to make pictures of their stones.

She thinks its a great story but something else makes her more curious.

"You said ZZ went out and came back with a suggestion."

"Yes, he did."

"Which was the same one you came up with."

"Yes, spooky, isn't it?"

"Richard, where did he get that idea from?"

"I don't know. Everytime we print late, he goes out for a walk, maybe to get a breath of fresh air or pee. He did that and I guess the idea came to him."

Even as I say that, I remember thinking how it is that ZZ always goes out when the music starts and returns when the music ends. But I have never mentioned the music to Jacqueline or anyone else and something tells me I should not now, not yet.

But her tone of voice suggests that maybe she suspects, suspects that I am not telling her everything, but she says nothing more.

Janice bounces up and asks how the pictures turned out. She's the stage manager for the production. Okay, I say, except the theme of death can't really be shown because the headstones won't print.

I feel a sharp kick on my shin and stop to look at Jac. Janice doesn't know anything about us yet and I'm not even on the subject, so I glance at Jac in surprise.

Janice says, it doesn't matter, just so long as we've got Fatso in costume and the whole thing looks like once upon a time in China. Catch you all for lunch, she says and runs off.

What's the kick for? I ask Jac.

"Don't talk about it."

"The picture?"

"Yes."

"Why not?"

"I don't know. It just doesn't feel good."

"You believe in these things?"

"Well, I don't, but my family does. You remember when we were staying out late for dinner all the time?"

66

"Could I forget?"

"Idiot. No, my mum wasn't too keen on it. I mean she's not really into the traditional beliefs and all, but it's sort of still at the back of her mind?"

"What is?"

"It was the Seventh Month."

"And?"

"Month of the Hungry Ghosts."

She is right. But it had been such a happy, wonderful time for me that all the ashes and candles on the roadside, the joss sticks, the little bowls of rice and plates of fruit for the hungry ghosts released from hell for a month had not made any impression on me.

"I mean, if my mum were really traditional, I would have been grounded the whole month."

"At least I got you home before nine."

"Such a dear."

ZZ believes in such things and I wonder if he also made the effort to get home early for dinner during that month. And as I was not there late with him, surely he would not have hung around till after the flute song? And if the flute-player, whoever it was, believed too, surely he or she would have high-tailed it home instead of playing late into the night in some dark, lonely stairwell?

Frame 21

"Do you think Jac will let you off one evening for our last club shoot for the year?" ZZ asks, almost shouting over the din of the drums and cymbals of the HJC Lion Dance Troupe in furious practice.

"I'll ask. But I think it should be fine," I shout back, laughing as the both of us work at the sink, watching the prints floating in their trays.

"It's something really close to our hearts, I believe. Our noisy neighbours helped us to get it together."

"What?"

"It's the birth of a lion."

"What?"

"The birth of a lion! There's a special ritual to bring a dancing lion to life."

"You mean that papier-mache head and blanket has a birthday ceremony?"

"Yes, and they take it pretty seriously too. You want to go shoot?"

"Hey, I think Jac might want to see this too. Can I bring her along?"

"Sure, just pay up her share for the bus ride."

The day comes and the club gathers in the school carpark to catch a ride on the bus that ZZ has chartered for us and the Lion Dance Troupe members. Jac and I are standing in a corner when I notice someone familiar, someone whom I haven't seen in the darkroom or at club outings for ages. Molly.

Hey, Molly! Long time no see! I call out to her, putting aside all her past hostility towards me. I'm too happy. It's a bright evening with a breeze, we're going somewhere to shoot and I've got the girl I love and my best friend with me. What could be better?

Hi, Richard, she says and actually smiles. Smiles. She doesn't look half bad when she smiles and since she's being friendly enough, I continue and ask, so where have you been? Haven't seen you on a club shoot for ages.

I joined the Chinese Orchestra, she says, and practice takes up a lot of time. But I've been shooting them too.

Then ZZ calls out all aboard and notices Molly and manages a polite smile.

I swear, she's nice to me now because I'm finally out of the way, I say to Jac, who laughs and says you're being an ass. No really, Jac, she's always seen me as a competitor for ZZ's attention. Notice how she smiled when she saw us? Hey, the moment she saw you with me, she must have put two and two together and realised we were going.

Are we? Jac asks sweetly.

Aren't we? I ask, alarmed.

You tell me.

We are. We most certainly are.

If you say it is, then it must be so and in a blatant infringement of school rules, she reaches out to take my hand and holds on all the way into the heart of Chinatown.

Frame 22

We stand hushed in the evening light in a tiny badminton-cum-volleyball court just off Neil Road. It's darker here than it really should be because the trees around the court are tall, and the walls of shophouses, covered with creepers, moss and mould, flank us on two sides.

It's been some time since we arrived early, and the people from the Chin Woo Athletic Association are just coming in from their day jobs and preparing themselves. It's an old club, ZZ says, founded in Shanghai in 1910 and just over 60 years old in Singapore. There are Chin Woos all over the world, he says, even in America and England, making that point particularly for me.

The Chin Woo members come out, dressed in the same kind of clothes I see our own Lion Dance guys wear, the tee shirt, the black trousers, the red sash and those shoes with the separate big toe. The Lion Dance chairman and ZZ go up to talk to a man, probably the Chin Woo leader and he's explaining something to ZZ in Mandarin, probably telling him what will happen so that ZZ can position the photographers.

Then the lifeless lion is brought out. We gather around the head while someone explains its inner workings.

Papier-mache, three-and-a-half kilos, he says, but always seems heavier than that.

It is dark by the time the troupe is ready, two men under the silk cape and papier-mache head. Dark and silent because much of the traffic is gone and because the lion lies dead still on a cracked concrete floor. The wind rustles in the big trees and tugs at the hairs on the lion's head whose eyes are sealed. It sees nothing, hears nothing, smells nothing, tastes nothing. Dead still.

Then the silence, the stillness of the evening is broken by the loud, clear voice of a man, the words of his Cantonese incantation carried on the breeze. With a paintbrush dipped in blood-red paint in his hand, he swiftly takes off the seal on the lion's left eye and touches the eye with paint, as if directing blood into a network of veins. Immediately, the eye lights up, just like a cat's in the dark, a glaring yellow orb in the dimly-lit courtyard.

With his brush, he spots the lion's ears and they wiggle to life. He touches the brush to its nose, its mouth, its beard and forehead and then runs the paint along its spine, calling out the parts as he works. The lion's body twitches to life.

Then the man looks up into the purple eveni14fic is shattered by the roaring of furious drums and the harsh clash of cymbals as the lion springs to its feet, swings its head around, mane catching the nightwind.

It begins to pace the court, stretching, hopping, pawing the ground, as if getting used to its body and limbs. Eyelids fluttering, the light in its eyes shine through translucent green lids. Then it moves forward slowly, moving towards the offerings on the ground. Joss sticks burn in a tiny brass pot filled with ashes behind two bunches of leafy vegetables with a red packet tied to each. Suddenly the lion lunges, head dropping to the ground and taking up the two bunches of greens in a single mouthful. With the greens and the treasures of the red packets in its belly, the lion now belongs to the Chin Woo. It washes its feet and begins to play, prancing to face North, South, East and West in turn.

The drumming and the clashing reach a climax and then, as if the spirit within the lion has decided to take its leave, the dancing suddenly stops, its life of dance begun.

It is late when we board the bus, and it is only when we're snuggled comfortably together does Jacqueline point out, dear, you never shot a single picture.

Frame 23

"You didn't shoot anything," ZZ remarks to me the next time we are in the darkroom. "How come?"

"Too caught up watching the lion coming to life. It never even occurred to me to lift the camera and shoot. It seemed so alive, like it was real, like it had its own personality, you know? I've never seen it like that before, not with our own troupe."

ZZ nods. "Fascinating, wasn't it? But the Chin Woo people have been doing it for ages. Like the man doing the head, he'd done it for twenty years, he told me. Our friends next door have only just begun to learn. Want some coffee?"

I stick out my tongue and shake my head. ZZ sighs as he prepares some D-76 for himself. A lot of spirituality in Chinese rituals, he says.

Like possession? I ask.

"That's a very negative way of looking at it."

But my own religion and culture have taught me that there is only one spirit that should reside in people. All others have no place there.

ZZ agrees. That's a very fundamental difference. It shapes the way we see the world.

"In your worldview," he says, "spirits are all evil but for one, the Holy Spirit. But like I told you before, in my worldview, spirits can be good or bad or some of both. Possession is also considered bad by us, but channelling, you know, when they have the medium, is not a straight out bad thing, because it allows us to communicate with our dead or with our deities, but we acknowledge that there is a bad element to it, because all mediums are doomed to die violently."

"So why do they even do it?"

"I don't know. Maybe they have no choice."

"So, er, have you ever spoken to a spirit?"

ZZ stares blankly at me for some time before he answers.

"I haven't been to see a medium to talk to my ancestors if that's what you mean."

Afraid that I might have offended him, I ask no more. He's gone tense, I can see it, but I can't understand. The last time we spoke about his ancestors, he was perfectly happy to talk about them. Change the subject, man, change the subject.

"I notice Molly's back."

ZZ smiles wryly "Yes, I noticed too."

"Did you speak to her?"

"No. Did you?"

"Yes. I asked her what she's been up to. She's been playing in the Chinese Orchestra."

ZZ raises his eyebrows. Really? they seem to ask.

"Yes. But I forgot to ask her what she plays. Probably

the erhu or something. Anyway, she looks happier now, less menstrual."

He laughs. "You're very mean to her."

"And what about you? The girl obviously likes you. And now that I'm not around you so often, she's trying to get close again but you're not responding."

"Responding to what?"

"Molly!"

"But she hasn't done anything."

"Hey, come on, the initiative has to come from the guy."

"Oh yes, and you showed loads of initiative with Jac, huh?"

"Well, not at the start, but now I do and I love every moment of it. You were right. It's nice to be in love."

ZZ laughs again, but he seems miles away from where we are.

"Religion is a very important thing," he says at last. "It doesn't just affect the way you see the world. It makes you what you are, gives you eyes that can see or can't see. Do you get that?"

"You mean it colours our view of the world, like filters?"

"No, no, something more basic than that even."

"Oh. Then maybe like between a telephoto or a wide-angle lens, angles of view?"

"No, not that either. Maybe format size. No, that's not it."

"Say, maybe the difference between normal film and infra-red?"

ZZ considers that and then nods slowly "Maybe, maybe that's it. Or maybe the difference between images created by reflected light or heat intensity."

"Then we're back to that old thing about being on different wavelengths, aren't we?" Even I know that much physics.

He nods slowly, but he is lost to the world.

Frame 24

I'm worried about ZZ, I tell Jacqueline at last and she asks why.

He's been having these moods. Gets kind of dreamy and distant. And this has been going on for a really long time, like from the time we started making prints. He disappears sometimes and when he comes back, he's dreamy. Or looks flushed and his eyes are bright.

Sounds like he's in love, she says. You should take a look at yourself sometimes.

"You mean I look as blur and lost?"

Jac looks up from her book and smiles sweetly. Yes you do.

"Well, then, you should never worry about whether I'm in love or not. You can tell just by looking."

"Yes, but I don't know if it's me you're in love with. Or someone else."

"So who am I in love with now?"

"Tell me."

"You, of course. But why do you keep wanting me to confirm it for you? You insecure?"

She narrows her eyes at me. "Don't insinuate things,

78

buster. I'm confident. I just want you to be sure. And if you can admit it to yourself, it's real."

"Brainwash."

"I don't need tricks to keep you," she says, brushing her hair back and smiling her magic at me.

"Oh, Mighty Mistress, I am your obedient slave."

"Now then, slave, what were you saying about your friend's dreaminess?"

I hesitate and wonder if I should tell her about the music and everything. It seems like such a weird idea in broad daylight, even though it's real enough at night to send me the shivers.

"Well, ever since I began to work in the darkroom with ZZ, we've been hearing this music late at night, well, not really too late, maybe eightish, nine-ish. It's a bamboo flute that plays some Chinese tune. The music's always different, but it's always kind of sad."

"And?" She is interested now, and closes her book.

"Well, always a little after the flute starts, ZZ leaves the darkroom for maybe half an hour, maybe an hour sometimes, I never keep track. When he comes back, he's always kind of funny, starry-eyed, dreamy. Then a little later, he says pack up and let's go."

"Almost like he's been waiting for the music?"

"Yes, now that you mention it. We don't always have to stay in so late, but we do. And we always leave right after he comes back, wherever he's been."

"Haven't you ever asked him about it?"

"No."

"Why not?"

Why not. I can't answer her. Maybe it is because I am always so busy — Chinese assignments, printing, whatever — that it never occurs to me to ask. Or maybe I just think it is a mood, the kind that sensitive, artistic people are prone too and ZZ is something of an artist with a camera. Maybe I do not dare intrude. Maybe I had not, simply had not linked the music and him. Or maybe I do not dare. And if the two are linked? What then?

"I don't know, Jac. I really don't know."

"Well, you're certainly close enough to him to ask. Is ZZ really terribly shy?"

"Yes, he is, rather. He practically hangs out only with me."

"Maybe he has a girlfriend you don't know about."

"What? Not possible! He would have told me."

"Look, what time does the watchman lock up the reading room?"

"About nine."

"And the music starts around nine. Early enough for someone else other than the two of you to be around, you know. So, the reading room closes at nine, which means everybody leaves the school and then the music plays. ZZ always disappears. Where else can he go but to whoever is playing the flute?"

"Wonderfully explained, Miss Marple. Now tell me why all the secrecy and funny music in the night."

"Well, maybe it's a relationship ZZ is not comfortable having other people know about. Maybe they both aren't comfortable about it, so they meet in school after everyone else has left. ZZ doesn't always go home with you, right?"

"What do you know, it might make sense after all. And he keeps it a secret from everyone, including me. He said the music has been going on since he was in first year, so this has been on for some time."

"Unless he said that just to throw you off."

"You mean it could be more recent?"

"I don't know. I've never heard the music."

"Do you want to stay up with me tonight to hear it?"

"What?"

"Yes, and when it starts, we'll sneak round to follow the sound and then we'll see who it is ZZ is having these secret meetings with."

"We will do no such thing. Richard, I'm surprised at you!" Jac says in mock anger. "This is your best friend. And if he's not ready to tell you about something, you should just leave it alone until he is."

"Which is when?"

"When he's good and ready."

Somehow, I do not see that any time soon.

Frame 25

Mooncake Festival's here, I say to ZZ one afternoon in the darkroom. Councillors have been stockpiling boxes and boxes of the stuff.

Mid-Autumn Festival, he corrects me. Who cares about the name? I laugh. I just want to stuff my face with mooncakes. We seldom get any at home, and if we do, my father picks a box of the cheapest variety and we hoard them, each of the four round cakes cut up into eight small pieces, making a total of 32. That makes six for each of us with one extra for the parents, but Henry invariably steals one and the last extra one is always offered to Elizabeth.

"You can come over to my place and eat all the mooncakes you want. I've got all types, from plain to double yolks to snowskin to durian flavoured. My family's really big on mooncakes," ZZ says.

"Heaven. This is going to be a great mooncake festival. The council is going to lay on a spread on the night itself. Then there's yours. And even Jac's mum said she'll be making some and I'm welcome to them."

"Hey! You've met her mum already?"

"Yes, sweet little old lady. Jac's the youngest daughter of three. The other two are married and moved out. Their dad died sometime back, so it's just Jac and her mum at home."

"I suppose having only daughters makes it easier to like even you," ZZ chuckles and I hit him.

"Hit me again and I won't tell you how you can impress Jac's mum."

"Oh? And how much more can I impress her?"

"Do you know the significance of the Mid-Autumn Festival?"

I shake my head.

"In the Chinese calendar, autumn falls on the seventh, eighth and ninth months. During the middle of the eighth, which is the middle of the season, the moon is supposed to be at the greatest distance from earth and is at its most luminous. We say that it is roundest at this time."

"Ah so the mooncakes. But I wish I could have them all year round. After all, there's a full moon every month, isn't there?"

"Pig. Anyway do you and Jac have any plans that night? Like joining the lantern walk?"

"Yes, we want to attend the school celebrations, then I'll have to take her home right after that."

"Okay then I won't roster you for shooting duty. Molly's just come to say she'd like to shoot that night."

"Molly?" I say, singing her name sweetly.

"Someone else is taking her place in the orchestra that night, so she's not needed to play," ZZ says, ignoring my tone of voice.

"And what does Molly play? I forgot to ask the last time."

"Molly? She plays the flute, I think."

Frame 26

I am so excited that I cannot concentrate on my Chinese lesson, not that I normally can anyway. Miss Chan notices my agitation and asks me what's wrong. In halting Mandarin, I try to tell her that I may have discovered who my best friend's secret love is. She laughs and I join her and anyone outside would think that Chinese remedials are great fun.

She has come to accept the fact that my ability in the language is little more than nothing and works on that basis with me. The assessment books I do can be done by a child in primary school — who's good at Chinese, of course. But still, I make mistakes. When we try the O-level exercises, I am still hopelessly lost and the times when I get more than half the answers right are the times when Jac helps me with the work. But my oral ability is going great guns, because Miss Chan refuses to translate anything into English for me and because Jac doesn't let her mother speak to me in any other language or dialect (but Auntie does when Jac's not within earshot).

There's no Mandarin spoken at my house for the simple reason that when the parents were in school, they had to learn English and Bahasa Melayu. Because English was the language of law and government and thus ascendant in the dark days before Independence, the parents did not think that Henry and I would ever need Chinese names and hence did not give us any. But when the Chinese electorate became important again and Mandarin was elevated, the parents bent with the political breeze and the sister was christened Elizabeth Young Shu Hui.

So why do you think you know who your best friend's secret love is? Miss Chan asks. She always asks questions in full sentences, often repeating parts of my earlier statements the correct way for my benefit.

It is the (I make the action of playing the flute) song that makes me think so. She plays the (action again), because when she plays, he goes to her. And this girl I know plays the flute (Miss Chan finally tells me the word). And she likes him. He is also very shy of her. So I think he likes her too. That's why I think it is she who plays the flute which he answers every night.

Miss Chan looks puzzled, as if she does not understand something and I think maybe my spoken Mandarin is still not so hot. You say she plays the flute. When does she play the flute?

She plays at night about the time when the reading room closes.

And he goes to her?

Suddenly I realise, that I may be giving something away, revealing a secret I am only guessing at but could be right about. ZZ would be so angry. My oral ability degenerates fast.

Well, I don't know, I mumble. We only hear the song. He is very happy whenever he hears the song.

Why do you two stay in school so late?

We work in the black room. We wash pictures there.

Have you ever seen the girl who plays the flute?

No, I say. In English, it sounds like I am telling the truth. But it is a plural 'you' that Miss Tan is using, meaning ZZ and I. But all I know is that he goes, and I don't know if he goes to see her. The flute player might not even be a girl, much less a girl that ZZ is in love with secretly.

No, we have not seen her. Unless she is the one I think she is.

Miss Chan nods, but the smile is gone from her face and we go back to working through answers for the multiple-choice section.

Frame 27

It is a Saturday afternoon, and I am in school to finish a history assignment. Jac has already gone home after a tough morning's training.

Saturday afternoons in school feel idyllic and it brings to mind long, lazy Saturday afternoons half a lifetime ago, when I had to attend catechism classes and miss the cartoons and Saturday matinee on television. The sun is hot, and the whole school, like the church we go to, is quiet except for the wind that carries dried up leaves scratching across the floor. I feel sleepy and peaceful and quietly contented, even happy that my assignment has brought me back for a day.

The Lion Dance people are not practicing today and then I remember that they and the Chinese Orchestra people have gone somewhere to perform, which explains the sweet Saturday silence. I stretch and yawn and feel the weight of my lids as the photostated sheets in front of me on the table in the forum swim out of focus.

The dream begins and I know it is a dream because of its oppressive heaviness and the feeling that I cannot get out of it. I know it is a dream because ZZ is talking rubbish, not making sense at all and so am I, the both of us in the darkroom making prints of pictures that for the life of me I cannot see. And there is no smell, no heavy pungent odour of D-76 and I know for sure that it is a dream, unless my nostrils have grown so used to D-76 that I can no longer detect it, even in dreams. We have our hands in chemicals and funny, I can feel the cold wetness of it, but not smell it and ZZ is talking and laughing, like we always do when the music starts and he stops talking to listen and I listen too, a jerky, halting melody of broken breathing that slowly grows more fluent, more fluid until the light shines in ZZ's eyes again. Give me a sec, he says, like he has so many other times before. Give me a sec and he goes away for what seems like a long time and the music just keeps playing, on and on and on and ZZ doesn't come back and I begin to wonder where he is and open the door of the darkroom — it is black outside — but the music plays on and I wonder where it's coming from, swirling in the night air, swirling in the darkness, swirling in my head, me seeing nothing until I force my eyes open and the light hits, blinding me.

Awake. But the music is still playing and I realise that this is not a dream. The music is on, and it is daylight, and I am here. There is no one else in the forum. Just me and the floating notes of the bamboo flute and I listen to it and it sounds like it is coming from one of the stairwells because it has a lovely echo. Getting up, my limbs are stiff and pins and needles stab at the arm that my head has been lying on. But the music draws me. Stairwell, left wing, extreme corner from where I am sitting.

I walk, then trot, then run towards the sound, afraid that it will suddenly stop and take the player with it. But the music plays on as I reach the bottom of the stairwell and step into a pool of light from the long, thin window opposite. At the foot of the stairs, the music is loud, and somehow, at this distance, it does not sound as sweet, as liquid as it always does when we hear it from a long way off at night. So close to the source now. I run up the flight of steps, turn and then see on the next flight, the figure of a girl sitting on the steps with a bamboo flute held to her lips, breathing out the notes that have haunted ZZ and me all these months. She hears me, turns, and I finally see her face.

Molly.

Frame 28

She looks up at me in surprise and I smile sheepishly. So it's you. I was wondering who it was that was playing.

Molly smiles and puts the flute down on a pile of books next to her. Yes, its me. I hope I didn't sound too bad.

"No, you sounded fine. A bit rougher than normal, but you sound fine."

"You mean you've heard me play before?"

"Well, I think it's you. The pieces sound the same. Some of it at least."

"It might be me then."

"You ever stay late in school?"

"Sometimes."

"I guess it is you we hear then."

She looks like she is about to say something and then decides not to and smiles.

"ZZ likes the sound of the bamboo flute a lot." I say and her eyes brighten.

"Does he really?"

"Yes. When we hear the flute at night when we're printing or something, he always goes out." I say, stressing the 'always'. "I guess he goes out to hear it better," I say with as much innocence as possible. And then I realise it might be true. I have never seen what ZZ does while he is outside the darkroom.

Molly holds up her flute and studies it.

"It's a really simple instrument," she says. "I mean simple in the way it's made. Just a hollow tube with holes. Nothing fancy."

"Yes, but it sounds really cool."

"I know, that's what drew me to it. I only learnt how to play it this year."

"Really? Who did you learn it from?"

"There's a guy in the Chinese Orchestra, Teck Seng, he's in the same faculty as ZZ, I think. He plays it really well and he showed me how. Then it was practice, practice, practice. Which is why I haven't been at club meetings and shoots."

"You play really well for a beginner."

"It isn't always me you hear. Probably Teck Seng."

"Uh-huh. Maybe ZZ goes out to talk to him or something. ZZ's really into all this Chinese culture stuff. Plus he's Taoist."

"He really likes the flute then?" she asks, looking thoughtful.

"Yep. No better way to his heart."

She laughs softly and blushes and I swear I have found ZZ's secret love.

Frame 29

Giant lanterns hang from the ceiling all along the ground floor of the left and right wings of the college, while a perfectly round moon hangs white in a velvet sky. All around us, people are lining up for lanterns or sticking little candles in them and starting to extend the concertinas of coloured paper. Councillors walk round with candles in their hands, lighting up the lanterns for the students.

"Richard, will you put away that mooncake?" Jacqueline says, exasperated. "You don't have to stuff your silly face now. Mum's got lots waiting for you later."

"Yes, dear," I say, putting down the slices of mooncake sitting on a serviette in my palm. We open up the lantern which I bought her, much bigger and fancier than those the councillors are giving out, but still cheap enough for me, though two dollars is still a day's meal.

We put in a candle, twist a stick round the wire and wait for the councillor to come with the fire. Tuck and Janice are already lighted up and are walking our way, their lantern glowing before them.

"I feel just like a kid again!" Janice shouts to us.

"My kid's more interested in mooncakes than me!" Jac shouts back and they laugh as they run up. Come on, let's get you lighted up, says Tuck, digging out a lighter from his pocket. He gets our candle going and I pull up the lantern around it, the paper glowing warmly from within.

"Oh, it's gorgeous," Jac says, slipping her arm through mine. "Thank you, Richard." The light is dancing in her eyes as she looks at me and says, "I'd like to kiss you, but you're just going to taste of mooncakes."

ZZ comes up just then and snaps a picture of us. How come you're alone, ZZ? He chuckles and says, what makes you think I don't have plans for later? She busy shooting other things for now? I ask in an insinuating tone. Jac goes ooooooh and ZZ blushes (I don't see it, but I bet he does).

It's just past eight by the time everyone's got their lanterns aglow and even some of the teachers are here with lanterns, Miss Chan included and I wave to her. The walk around the school is about to start when suddenly I hear the music. ZZ hears it too and looks up and frowns and checks his watch.

"Way cool," Janice says. "Even the right music for atmosphere. The councillors think of everything!"

I scan the crowd, looking for the telltale flashes, but although I see the other club photographers, Molly isn't anywhere around. I snigger and nudge Jac. Romantic rendezvous time. Looks like she's too early. Couldn't wait I guess. Jac is saying don't be wicked when ZZ suddenly leaves us, walking quickly in the direction of the darkroom.

"This is a great time to catch him red-handed," I say, but Jac keeps a tight grip on my arm.

"Tonight's for me," she says, sounding petulant, and in the darkness, I steal a quick kiss, lips just brushing her smooth cheek. Pacified, she leans on me and I feel a quiet sense of completeness and contentment.

Then, as the great snake of light uncoils to move, the music suddenly stops and a horrible scream pierces the balmy, moonlit night. Everyone looks up, suddenly hushed and then, murmurs and people talking. ZZ appears from somewhere near the top floor and shouts, councillors! Councillors! Get a stretcher! Someone's fainted up here!

Most of the lanterns have gone out when the lights of the ambulance and police car flash red blue red blue red blue red blue, sweeping round and round like beacons on the brown walls of the buildings. People are talking, but in hushed, worried tones, all the festive feeling gone. ZZ is answering questions from a policeman and the nursing officer is injecting sedative in Molly's arm to stop her from screaming and thrashing around in her restraints on the stretcher. Miss Chan is discussing something with the teachers, and she looks troubled.

"Richard, I'm really scared," Jac whispers and I keep my arm tight around her while next to us, Janice is crying and asking what's going on here.

I'd answer her if I could. Really, I would.

Frame 30

ZZ doesn't know what happened either. Or if he does, he's not telling me.

I went up to see who was playing the flute, he says. And also to see if I could get a shot of the people downstairs, all in one long line of lighted lanterns.

I went up to the top, past the darkroom level, following the sound. I had to get up higher too, because the lens I had on wasn't wide enough to get everything.

When I got there, the music was strong, but I saw no one until I heard Molly screaming and saw her fall on the floor. I ran to her, saw that she had fainted and then started shouting for the councillors to come up.

It's hard for me to say, but I manage, and the words come out strained. I thought you went up to meet Molly. I thought you knew it was her playing the flute.

No, no, I didn't know it was Molly. I never expected her there at all. I mean, I never even knew she played the flute until recently, when she asked if she could shoot that night.

Yes, I say, the police found her camera. But they never found the flute. She must have dropped it and it rolled away or something.

ZZ looks at me and says, I honestly don't know what happened.

ZZ, do you know who plays the flute every night when we're here in the darkroom? He stares at me for a moment before he answers. No I don't, he says, in a tone that says it's final. No I don't. I don't. And for the first time in our friendship, I think that he is lying to me.

Where do you go when you leave the darkroom? I ask and this makes him angry.

Richard, you're my best friend, he says, the pain in his eyes for real and I feel immediately sorry for asking that and apologise.

What are you thinking, Richard? he asks. What are you thinking? That Molly and I have had something on all these months? That it's her who's been playing at night, calling me out for some secret meeting? Is that what you think, Richard? And that what happened last night is my fault? That I said or did something to upset her and she freaked out? Is that what you think? Is it?

I don't know what to think because you're not telling me everything. But everything he's just accused me of thinking makes sense in a frightening way. It seems so plausible, so real.

I can't judge, I say at last.

Then don't, ZZ sighs. Don't judge me. I swear, Richard, you have to believe me, I have nothing to do with Molly and I don't know what the hell she was doing on the fourth level playing the flute in some dark corner. If nothing else, just believe this because it's the truth.

Then it hits home, hits home so hard that I want to cry. Oh my God, my God, is it my fault? For telling Molly all those things about the flute player and how ZZ always responds to it? My knees go weak suddenly my whole body feels weak. Maybe she has nothing to do with the flute we hear every night. Maybe she just heard what I said and then no no no just decided to do it herself, be the flute player that we heard to draw ZZ to her. Just to bring him to her. Because she had some silly crush on him. Her flute brought ZZ, alright, but what else did it bring?

What's wrong? ZZ asks.

Everything, man, everything. I tell him about Molly, my head spinning and ZZ stays silent throughout, his eyes staring blankly at the wall.

It isn't Molly, he whispers at last. It isn't. He looks at me and I've never seen him sadder.

There's something I need to tell you, Richard. I've told no one, and I don't know how to tell you.

Take your time, I say, we got time.

Can you wait with me?

We wait. The clock hands move; five, six, seven, eight, nine, ten. And I realise that for the first time since I started working in the darkroom, I have not heard the song of the bamboo flute.

Frame 31

The nights are silent, again and again and again. And if ZZ had not insisted that Molly was not the flute player, I would have been convinced that it was her.

No one knows what happened to Molly that night. She just cries a lot in the day and when night comes, she is afraid to sleep and refuses to let the nurses turn out the lights. That much we know.

Word starts to go round that maybe the school is haunted, that maybe Molly saw a ghost and it shocked her so bad she's in her present state.

Jac's mother will not let her stay late now and since I see her home, I start leaving the college while it's still light too. And ever since the flute song ended, ZZ doesn't seem so eager to stay up late so often, not even to study in the reading room. Or maybe it's just because his A-levels are coming and he's getting down to serious work. But he never tells me the thing he was about to tell me the night after Molly's accident, when the flute song never came.

We don't talk about it either. It's unsettled and that's the way we've let it rest between us. Our meetings in the darkroom are also brief, when we go in and out during the day. It feels like something has changed between us, but I try to tell myself that its just the exams, his A-levels and my promotionals, that are moving us apart and that it's only for now.

Then one day, after having spent the better part of the afternoon with Jac at her place, I remember a file I need and it's in the darkroom, left there when I went in to do some work in the morning. I have a key myself and don't need ZZ to open the door for me. Not planning to go to school the next day, as all classes have officially ended and we are free to stay at home and mug, I decide to get the file back that evening.

It's almost nine when I reach the darkroom and already, people are leaving the reading room. I go up quickly to the darkroom and to my surprise, the light is on and ZZ's things are there, but he's nowhere around. Finding my file, I don't leave immediately, but wait for ZZ to come back, but he doesn't. So I go out into the lab, into the corridor where I can see the backs of the stragglers as they make their way across the pitch black school field to the bus-stops at Bukit Timah and Dunearn Roads.

I want to call out his name, but something holds my tongue and then I hear a murmuring, a voice, somewhere above me. The stairwell is still open. Old Liew, the watchman, doesn't close up until half-past nine, when he's absolutely sure no one else is in the building. Quietly, I tiptoe up the stairs, the silence making me conscious of every sound my shoes make, the swish of uniform fabric, the tik-tik of the zipper pulls of my haversack and the passing of the faint smell of chrysanthemums through my nostrils.

A murmur, a soft laugh. One more flight of stairs and I hear a soft rhythmic thump, of something soft, yet hard, bumping against something. At the top of the stairwell, I edge towards the corner of the exit, keeping in the shadow and looking out, looking into where the ECA rooms are and I see a familiar figure, just the silhouette, sitting on a table, leaning against a pillar, swinging a leg, his rubber heel tapping against the leg of the table.

ZZ's talking, softly, and I can't hear what he's saying. He laughs, softly again, and the tone of his voice is gentle, like a lover's. He says something again, pauses, nods his head and goes on, all the time swinging his foot while I try to breathe silently the air now heavy with the odour of chrysanthemums, burning in my nose like incense.

It's dark, and it's some time before my eyes adjust totally and the shapes become clearer, but no matter where I look around him, no matter how I place my eyes, I cannot, just cannot see who ZZ is talking to. Nothing else is moving but his head, his hands, his leg.

He's just there, alone in the night, talking, laughing, as if to someone, but totally alone, swinging his leg.

Something deep inside makes me want to scream, want to turn and run because I don't understand what I'm seeing — or not seeing. But I check myself, move back slowly, back deeper into the shadows, when ZZ's foot stops swinging and he turns his head my way, trying to see into the shadow. I go down the stairs, as quickly and as quietly as I possibly can, all the way down the eternity of four floors until I am on the ground, stepping out into the moonlit plaza, walking briskly across the red-bricked circle, my backpack bouncing on my back, then reaching the sweeping flight of granite steps, trotting down them, faster and faster until I reach the bottom and feel the grass beneath my shoes and I can't control myself a moment longer and break into a run, just run, run, run across the neverending field for all I'm worth, away from school, away from ZZ, away from everything I cannot understand and away from that oppressive sweet stench of chrysanthemums that stays on my clothes and in my head.

Frame 32

Henry wakes, surprised to see me sleeping in our room, something I have not done for some time. He does not say anything and rises to get ready to go to the uni. I am so scared by the events of the night that I don't want to sleep alone outside, in the dark of our panel van. And for once, I am glad for Henry's company.

At breakfast, no one notices my presence as usual, but even so, I am grateful for the feeling of everything being business as usual and nothing out of the ordinary; and then we get up to go our separate ways, the father to his shop, mother to market, Henry to Kent Ridge, Elizabeth to the Convent, me to Jac's home where a second breakfast waits.

When I see her, it's about all I can do to prevent myself from crying out of sheer frustration at my helplessness. She just holds me at the door, my head on her shoulder, and her mother comes out of the kitchen to see what's the matter.

Something's wrong with his best friend, mum. Jac's mum sits me down and asks what I would like to drink and I tell her anything, Auntie and then remember, anything but chrysanthemum tea.

What's wrong with ZZ? Jac asks and I tell her about how I went back to school and found the darkroom open.

Auntie's back from the kitchen with a cup of Milo and she sits to listen as I recount the night's events.

When I finish, Auntie shakes her head and says it isn't normal. I say it can't ever be normal to talk to yourself like that in the dark, to talk as if someone else is there and answering you. No, she says, that alone would be reason enough to worry. And then she says the thing I have been trying so hard, so hard not to even consider, just trying to tell myself that ZZ is nuts and stressed and that's why he's talking to himself.

It isn't normal to talk to spirits, she says and the words cut deep and I shudder in Jac's arms even though it's broad daylight and I have two people I love with me.

What kind of boy is he? she asks, and I tell her and Jac tells her. I tell her about his home, his beliefs, his altar and ancestral tablets and the conversations we have about God and ancestors and spirits and how he's so afraid of making them ashamed of him.

He really believes? she asks and I nod. She looks at me and then says, I come from a family background like your friend's, except that by the time my generation grew up, most of us no longer believed in it and we don't perform the rituals anymore. But some things, like not staying out after dark during the Seventh Month and all that, some things we still believe. It's very deep and hard to forget.

The question sticks in my throat but I have to ask.

Auntie, does he just believe he is talking to a spirit or is he actually talking to one?

She shakes her head and says, I don't know. Even for believers, it is not normal to talk to the spirits like that, like as if they are here. Oh, Jac will tell you, when Uncle first died, I missed him so much and I would have given anything to have been able to talk to him, but nothing like that ever happened to me. Maybe because my beliefs are not strong, I don't know. But it is not a normal thing to talk to people on that side. If your friend can see them and talk to them, maybe he has what the older folks call a third eye. But that means he doesn't just see one person. He sees all.

The horror of it. The pure, mind-numbing horror of it. What did ZZ see that I did not when we worked late at night? What did he see in those pictures of the headstones that I didn't? What did he see sitting beside him in the dark that I could not?

But it was daylight, Auntie's Milo was still hot and Jac's arm was warm around my shoulders. And my best friend was either going insane or stuck somewhere, caught between the worlds of the living and the dead.

Auntie, I say at last, how can I help him?

Frame 33

Another day passes, then another and another. I haven't heard from ZZ and I haven't been down to school either. I don't know if I'm just too scared to confront him or maybe I just have no idea of what I'm going to say to him. Either way, I'm frozen.

It's a whole week before I don't smell chrysanthemums where they aren't, a whole week before I can walk home in the dark again. But I'm still sleeping in the room with Henry. Then one bright morning, I call Jacqueline to tell her I'm off to school to check on ZZ first before going up to her place.

The air-con of the darkroom is humming and I know that he is in there. When I push open the door, it's pitch black and I fumble for the switch. The yellow light clicks on, filling the room with warm, dim light and ZZ is sitting in a corner, staring at me, staring past me in the artificial forever night of the darkroom.

"Are you afraid of the dark?" he asks. His voice is soft, controlled.

"No more than you should be."

"Haven't seen you in school."

"Been studying."

ZZ doesn't move from his seat and from where I'm standing. I can see that he's been crying. There are tear stains on his face and his eyes are red.

"Why did you run away, Richard?"

"I couldn't handle it."

ZZ nods.

"What were you thinking?" he asks.

My mind is clear now. "I thought you were nuts."

"That's all?"

"Maybe possessed."

He nods again. "Reason enough to run away. So, have you decided what it is I am? Nuts or possessed?"

"I don't know. You tell me."

"I'm neither, Richard. Right now, I'm just broken." He smiles weakly, his gaze never moving from my face.

"You need help, ZZ."

"And are you here to give it?"

"As far as I can, yes."

"So what do you plan to do?" He looks right into my eyes, his tear-filled, bloodshot eyes that look like they have not slept for a week, just weeping, weeping, weeping.

"I don't know. I don't even know what the problem is, ZZ."

He pats his chest, right over the heart.

"Don't you know what its like to love someone?"

"I do now."

"Don't you want to know who it is I've been loving all this while, Richard?"

"Tell me."

He is silent for a long time, as if preparing himself to take me on a leap of logic, a leap of faith to another plane of existence.

"Feng. Her name is Chun Feng. Spring Breeze."

But it is only a name, and I can see her as clearly as I can see the wind.

"And what does she look like?"

"Haven't you seen her, Richard?"

"I saw only you, not her."

"She's got short hair," he says, putting his hand near his collar. Dark eyes, but bright and fair skin. She's seventeen now. Was seventeen when we met last year. Will be seventeen next year and after that too.

"Where's she from?"

"From here, like we are."

"And how did you meet?"

"When I was alone one night, working in the darkroom and I heard her playing the flute. I went up to look and saw her and we started talking."

"And you went up almost every night after that."

ZZ nods. He smiles, sadly.

"I always wondered why you never asked me too much about it."

He moves in his seat and I find another one to sit down in, and we sit, facing each other, sitting at each end of the darkroom, talking across its length, still a world away from each other.

"I didn't realise what it was about her. I thought she

was just another girl who liked to stay up late. But then she never let me walk her home and slowly she told me about herself."

"And what did she tell you?"

"She died a few years ago. Took her own life because she was sick and the doctors couldn't cure her."

"How did you react?"

"Like you, I guess."

"So why did you keep going back?"

"Because by then I'd grown to love her."

I do not know what to say. ZZ hasn't managed to make me take that leap of logic and faith with him. It is clear now. We're standing on opposite sides of a gap that I can't cross and he won't come back over. It is a long time before I can even ask another question.

"Remember what you once told me about loving an image instead of a real person?"

ZZ glares at me. You don't get it. You just don't get it, do you. He sighs. How long must I suffer fools?

"She isn't a part of my imagination, Richard. So you can strike off that idea that I might be nuts. Didn't you love Sam once, Richard? Wasn't she only an idea even though she was physically present?" His voice is dangerous now. And his eyes are angry.

I never loved Sam, I remind him.

"Remember how you told me it was better to love someone real, and possible, like Jacqueline, and not some fantasy like Samantha?"

ZZ nods.

"Then why did you let yourself love this fantasy?"

He looks up at me and snorts, shaking his head. His voice is louder, harder, and he is leaning forward in his chair to glare at me.

"She isn't a fantasy to me, Richard. She's real, she's as real as you and me. As real as you sitting there and looking at me and talking to me. She has a name, a face, a family. She had a life, Richard, just like you and me. She had a life until that damned disease killed her kidneys and her father couldn't pay the bills to keep her alive."

"Don't you remember that story I told you, Richard? About the girl who gave up her life for her father? Why do you think I told that to you? Didn't you think it had some meaning for me? Real meaning?"

His words are registering. I know what he is talking about, everything makes sense, but I don't understand. She is real. He isn't talking to himself. She is real. Or at least he thinks she is. Utterly and totally convinced she is. I find my voice.

"ZZ, even if she's real and she's there, you shouldn't be seeing her because it isn't normal."

"By whose standards?" he snaps, his voice sharp.

"Mine, and yours and everyone else's."

He laughs, cynically at first, and it grows, grows until he is hysterical and I am afraid.

ZZ, cut that out.

But he goes on. Laughing, laughing, laughing.

What's normal, Richard? Tell me, what's real and what isn't? Tell me, what's real? He's crying and laughing and crying and laughing and I think he's really lost it and I panic.

ZZ, I start to shout. Stop that. Then anger cuts in like a shield to protect me from my fear and I stand up, push my way through the chairs, reach for ZZ's collar and haul him to his feet. My strength surprises me. I have not felt such anger, such total, helpless anger before, not when my parents punished me for something I never did, not when Henry stole my food or pocket money, not when Elizabeth gave me her cheek and I couldn't do anything about it. And now all the rage I'd kept deep inside is rising up and all I can see in front of me is ZZ and his laughing crying mocking face. Will you wake up, I yell and slam him against the metal cupboard. He whimpers and I drop him to the floor, then bend over him and haul him up again and he is still laughing and I let fly with my palm, let him take a loud, hard slap across the face and he is still laughing and crying but doing nothing to defend himself. Then I let him crumble into a heap.

I turn around and I remember little after that because everything is a blur, a smashing light-bulb, a chair flying across the pitch black room at me and me floundering in the dark, catching hold of ZZ's collar and cutting myself on his school badge then slamming my fist into his face, just hitting, hitting every part of him with everything in me. Then my fingers find the safelight switch and with a click, everything is bathed in the blood-red glow of the light and ZZ's nose is bleeding and already his eye is swelling. And he's still crying.

I can't go back to her, Richard. I can't, he sobs and I walk over cautiously, half expecting a sudden attack from him, crouched in a corner like a tortured kitten.

You don't have to, ZZ, I say, as gently as I can, as breathless as I am. It's over. You don't have to.

He shakes his head. You don't understand, Richard. I love her and I want to go back to her. But I can't. She's gone Richard, she's gone. She left the night you saw us and I've been waiting for her every night since, but she's gone. His breathing comes in gasps, his body trembling like a leaf.

She's gone, he sobs. And I take him in my arms, his head resting on my shoulder like a baby, blood soaking the beige fabric of my uniform.

She's gone, he sobs.

She's gone.

Frame 34

Jacqueline tells me it's not my fault, but how can it not be? It was me who was stupid enough to assume it was Molly playing the flute and give her ideas about being the flute player. It was me who was so much of a coward I didn't dare go back to help my best friend. A week. He was alone a whole week, just sitting there and crying in the dark. How can it not be my fault when I could have gone back so much earlier? To get him out of the blackness before something snapped inside him?

Jac's been very patient, very understanding, but even so, the strain is starting to show. We spend a lot less time together now and I spend a lot of the year end holidays at ZZ's bedside in hospital where he doesn't talk, doesn't move, just stares at the wall in front of him, like as if none of us is there.

When he's moved home, I visit once, twice, until his family sort of suggests I should not be there anymore. I think they blame me. I've heard relatives asking why Zhuang Zi's best friend never warned his parents about his possession. Why his best friend never went to help until it was too late.

But can't they see that my eyes see another world quite different from theirs?

But even if I just thought that ZZ had a nervous breakdown and never saw the girl he calls Chun Feng, maybe something in the back of my mind understood, understood everything we'd talked about and the things ZZ believed in and did and it frightened me so much that I ran.

If all I thought was that ZZ was nuts from exam pressure, surely I would have gone right up to him to say hello, isn't it time to go home? Then brought him home, made sure he was safe, told his parents. That's what a good friend — a best friend — would have done.

But I did nothing like that. I ran away. Didn't do anything to help him. Didn't warn his parents. Just ran away like a little coward too frightened to help his friend. Didn't help until it was too late.

At least Molly's better, Jac tells me. Someone says she left hospital in time to repeat her first year in another school. Her grades weren't good, a teacher says. She wouldn't have made it through the promotionals and that's probably what made her crack. They say she's pretty much normal now, except she won't go anywhere dark alone and its like a slice of time has just disappeared from her mind. She doesn't remember anything about that night and no one wants to ask.

I am trying to forget it too. But I do ask Miss Chan about the whole thing one last time, because she seemed so perturbed when I first mentioned it, and she seemed so worried that mid-autumn night. She sighs and tells me she had a pupil some years ago who could play the flute beautifully. She became ill and killed herself so that she would not burden her poor father, who was a lorry driver. I am not saying she haunts the school, Miss Chan warns me, or that she was responsible for what happened that night, but we should not be too curious about the other world.

It's enough for me and I leave it at that.

When the new year starts, Jac and I don't stay late and on the few occasions that I do, I listen for the flute in fear, wanting to hear it, yet hoping I won't. Especially when the Lunar New Year comes and the councillors hang up a giant red diamond with the Chinese character *chun*, which means spring. And I think it looks like a sign to call her spirit home, but it's hung upside down, like the character *fu*, luck, is hung outside people's doors. I ask a councillor why the *chun* is upside down and he isn't sure, but he remembers his grandmother saying something about it being hung that way to either ward away bad luck or confuse evil spirits. I shudder at the thought of the return of Chun Feng's ghost, and in the evenings while the decorations are up, I half expect to see a girl with a flute walking among the cherry blossom branches the councillors have made and stuck around the balustrades.

It follows too that I don't print pictures or even go near the darkroom anymore and the Seagull sits at home in an old Tupperware box with a few sachets of silica gel.

Frame 35

Then one day, Jacqueline asks: how are we going to cele-brate Valentine's?

We've been together just past half a year now and we've already slipped into patterns of coming to college and attending classes together, doing our work together in the forum, moving around together but not really with each other.

It isn't her fault. She's the same wonderful girl I became friends with and fell in love with. She's still bright and cheery, laid back and loving. But you've changed, she says, and I know what she means. I've almost all but with-drawn from the rest of the class, even Janice and Tuck. And if I'm not with Jac, I'm somewhere on my own, any-where where it's quiet and I don't have to deal with the noise and movement of this world.

So we need some quality time together, she says and I laugh. You make us sound like we're married. That would be quite nice, she says and I feel a welling of warmth and tenderness for her. Do you want a ring?

She sighs and kisses me on the cheek. Will you keep running off on your own, avoiding everyone but me?

It's nobody's fault, dear, just mine.

When will you forgive yourself?

I don't know. When it feels right to, I guess.

Valentine's is not marked in school. The councillors are told not to make an event of it and the principal calls it a western tradition that has no place in our college. But still the boys come to school with roses and girls walk around with single stems or big bouquets and heart-shaped boxes of chocolates while cards are passed around openly or slipped quietly into files, an underground celebration that just about everyone in school has a part in, whether it's a quiet dinner for two or a class outing of lonely hearts.

My heart aches to see Jacqueline go through the day without a bouquet because I have no roses for her. They cost so much more on Valentine's and I've been saving for her present and our dinner. But she understands and when we get to school that morning, the first thing she does is take me to the stairwell where her locker is to kiss me quickly and pop a chocolate into my mouth and say she can't wait for dinner.

It's evening and Jac and I head for Coronation Plaza for a dinner fit for royalty, she jokes. There's a little cafeteria on the second floor, tucked right away into a far end corner that sells the best *hor fun* Jac and I have ever tasted. They've got those old time high-backed seats too, the kind you find in really old *kopi-tiams* that call themselves Milk Bars or Bars and Family Restaurants. So we walk there, holding hands even though we're both in uniform, get ourselves a corner table with the high-backed seats and order our main meal. It's our best dinner ever, because it's been so long since I've been 'all here' with her, as Jac puts it.

But a cafeteria needs its tables and a meal doesn't last too long, so we're out within the hour and I say to Jac, shall we take a really nice, slow walk home? Then as we step out into the night, a chilly wind blows and dark clouds go rolling across the sky.

Oh no, she cries. It's going to pour and if we take a bus home, we'll be back in no time at all. We could sit here and wait out the rain, I suggest and she says, no, I've got a better idea. I've always wanted to do this. What? I ask, but she doesn't say anything, just takes my hand and pulls me along, back towards college.

Its half past nine and the reading room has long been closed, the shutters of the stairwells drawn. The plaza isn't totally dark, because the forum lights are on and when we get to the middle of the red-bricked circle, Jac puts down her bag and takes out her Walkman, the first of its kind, which has double-jacks for headphones. We listen to music pretty often together when we're in the forum or on the bus, but this is different, Jac says. I've always wanted to do this, but there were always too many people around. She clips the Walkman to my belt, plugs in for both of us and then as Manilow begins, your eyes are sad eyes, and mine are too, she steps into my arms and I close my arms around her.

The wind is blowing harder now, but I don't feel it, only feeling the warmth of her arms around my neck and

117

her body so close to mine I can feel her heart beating against my chest. Then when Manilow asks wouldn't it be sad being lonely all alone, the first drops of rain begin to fall and laughing, we pick up our bags and go into the forum, lit by the yellow globes of light on the pillars.

The rain falls harder and harder, louder and louder, until the rest of the world doesn't seem to exist, just Jac and I, in each other's arms, moving slowly to music no one else can hear, the world cut off by a shimmering curtain of rain.

Can't it always be like this, she asks when we stop to change tapes. I want to tell her that it can, but I know now that things change, people change and the best that we can do is deal with the change, grow with it, make room for it. I want to tell her that, but I don't know how to, don't know how to tell it because I don't know how to do it.

The tape starts rolling and with a smile, she puts her arms around me again. We stand for a long time like that, neither saying anything, just holding on to each other until I say, remember the ring?

What? You actually got it? You shouldn't have, I thought we agreed that I'd only let you buy me dinner, she says and I know she means it. But I began saving for it from the time we started going out and now, it shines in the dim yellow light, a simple band of pale gold with our initials — RY+JN — inscribed inside. It slips easily onto her ring finger and she laughs, never mind, it gives me space to get fat. Then she reaches round her neck, unclasps the thin chain with the little heart of gold and puts it around my neck and it barely fits.

Sweetheart, your mum gave this to you.

She'll understand. She's given me others.

I love you, darling.

I love you too, she says softly. I always will.

I still hear those words as clearly as if Jacqueline is here with me now, whispering it into my ears as she did that night.

When the rain finally eases, it is almost eleven and we walk out slowly our shoes getting wet in the puddles of water that line the rough path to the little gate next to Chinese High's big one. Holding her left hand, I can feel the ring, loose on her finger, feel the odd sensation of the fine chain around my neck, feel the warmth of her arm pressed against mine.

Something's behind us now and we're both happy and we don't need to say anything as we cross the overhead bridge to Dunearn Road, the lights of cars and lamps all making the rain-wet streets glisten. I will try to forget about things past. I will try to forgive myself for them. And be glad in the love of a wonderful girl who just wants to be mine. We're off the bridge and on the road and I'm on the outside, trying to protect her from the spray thrown up by passing cars. But I never see the one that makes her scream, makes her swing me around with all her athlete's strength, throwing me into the shallow drain as the car climbs the kerb and hits her, sending her body tumbling over the bonnet and smashing through the windscreen.

I can only remember crying her name, struggling to get out of the drain, hands dragging me out, hands holding me back from where Jacqueline lies and then the flashing of red and blue lights and the growing blackness from the searing pain in my skull.

Frame 36

When I wake, it is too late to even see Jac one last time.

They say she was dead on arrival, Elizabeth tells me. Dead on arrival. A heartless, factual description of the end of a life so precious. I start to cry and tell myself they aren't Elizabeth's words. She's only thirteen and doesn't yet understand how even neutral words can cut so deeply. And she doesn't know the total helplessness of knowing there's really nothing that you can do but cry.

It's a long while before Elizabeth says anything again and I realise that she's still there.

"Richard, don't cry," she pleads, her own eyes red. Then she holds out something in her palm and says, "I didn't know you had a girlfriend." It's Jac's chain, the one with the little gold heart and she puts in my hand.

"Yes, I did, Liz." The feel of the chain in my hand and my own past-tense description of Jac's place in my life brings fresh tears.

"Her mother came to see you," she says and my heart breaks.

"She wanted to tell you she doesn't blame you."

"Does she know how Jac died?"

"The people at the bus-stop saw her push you away."

"And Auntie doesn't blame me?"

"She said she'll see you when everything's over."

When everything's over.

"Has Jac?" I cannot bring myself to say it.

Elizabeth nods. "I went with her family to Mount Vernon this morning."

A body so warm, so tender, so full of life, so full of Jacqueline. So full of love. Nothing now but ashes. Just ashes.

"Why didn't anyone wake me?"

"You're concussed."

She moves to tidy the things on the little bedside table.

"You've been in and out of consciousness for four days. I wanted to wake you, shake you or something, but mum and dad wouldn't let me," she says at last.

"Thank you."

She smiles weakly, "I thought you might have wanted to see her."

"I do still."

"Your classmates came too," she quickly adds, "and this tall, skinny guy. He just sat by your bed and talked to you, even though you weren't saying anything back."

"Did he say who he was?" but I already know.

"No, he just told me to take care of you because he was going away and couldn't do it anymore."

"Did he say where he was going?"

"No. But he cried when he said goodbye."

Frame E

The light is fading, the shadows growing. The voices have grown softer until I can no longer hear them.

I have not been back to college since that Valentine's. My Chinese, exam results came out while I was still on medical leave and there was no need to go back to school, not that I wanted to anymore, anyway.

The army claimed me that June and my parents thought it would be a good way to help me forget and get out of the private, silent world I had locked myself into. But no matter where I was, I sought the quiet, lonely places where I could speak out loud, where only Jacqueline and no one else could hear me. It did not matter that she never replied. I did not expect her to.

All I needed was to talk to her: to tell her how I missed her, tell her what I was doing in the army, tell her how I'd fared in my first, second and third attempts at my A-levels, tell her that I'd actually made it to the university because they relaxed the rules on Chinese, tell her how her mother was, tell her about Elizabeth's first date and tell her that I still loved her very much and always would.

And somewhere during all that, I began to understand

what ZZ had been doing. Except he said that he could hear her talking back.

It would have been good, I think, if Jac had talked to me, somehow. To chide me, to comfort me, to cheer me on. Sometimes, out in the field, sleeping next to my radio set, the rush of static would break and for a moment, I would hope that it would be her voice calling to me over the ether. But of course, she never did. And I guess its just as well. I can't bear the thought of her spirit drifting between both worlds with nowhere to rest.

I am standing now in the old forum, the one where I last held Jac and told her that I loved her and heard her replying, I love you, I always will and her words are clear now, as if she is right here beside me, telling me herself. But she is not in these arms and I feel the wrenching emptiness of her absence and start to cry.

But I am here, I hear her say. I am here in your heart forever, and in the heart you can no longer wear around your neck that's grown too thick. I am here in the photographs you took of me, here at the table we sat at, here where we danced on our last night together, here in every place we've ever been because you remember everything so clearly. Here, even though you cannot see me.

ZZ, I say, I understand you now. I really understand now. And this time, my tears are for him and a girl named like the wind. With sorrow, my fear disappears and slowly, I head for the darkroom. When I get there, the door is open, the furniture gone, the silence overwhelming. Two more floors up, all the way to the night I found ZZ sitting alone and there is only the wind. I watch the light fading in the sky and then go back downstairs.

When I reach the forum, a patrol car pulls into the carpark and a pair of policemen step out. One of them waves to me, a Corporal with a belly who looks like he might have children still in school. He walks down the brick steps where I have seen heavy rain throw a veil of mist and spray over, the water cascading down the steps like a waterfall. The policeman walks across the forum to where I am standing.

"Hello," he says. "Are you an old student?"

"Yes, I am."

"Sorry about your school," he says, looking up at the forum's high ceiling.

"It's okay. We'll manage somehow."

"Nice place, too bad they'll have to tear it down. One of my nieces came here," he says. "Are you going to stay much longer?"

"No. I'll be going in a few minutes."

"Okay we're here to make sure nobody comes in. It's not safe anymore, you know."

"I know." Something in my voice gives me away.

"A lot of memories?" he asks, more gently.

"A lot."

He nods, almost knowingly.

"Finished NS?"

"Just. I'm waiting for university to start."

The policeman smiles and then sighs.

"You have a good life ahead of you. Make it count."

I am surprised a stranger is saying this to me and he goes on, "I hope your memories of this place are happy, but if they're not, don't let them hold you back. Life goes on, yah?"

He smiles. I smile and something clicks in my memory and my heart soars, making me want to just call out Jac's name.

"Thank you, officer. I'll be going now. But I need to do one last thing before I go."

"Go ahead," he smiles, patting my back and turning to walk back to his waiting patrol car.

From my haversack, I take out the bouquet I couldn't afford to buy Jacqueline that Valentine's, kiss it and place it, slightly crushed, on the little space where we danced.

Goodbye, darling, I know you want me to go, I whisper.

Thank you for telling me I can.

But I'll always love you. I always will.

Then I walk away from the world we shared, back into my own, alone, the photographs still dancing with the wind.